Robyn Donald

THE ROYAL BABY BARGAIN

By Royal Command

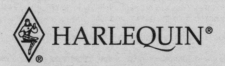

HARLEQUIN®

TORONTO • NEW YORK • LONDON
AMSTERDAM • PARIS • SYDNEY • HAMBURG
STOCKHOLM • ATHENS • TOKYO • MILAN • MADRID
PRAGUE • WARSAW • BUDAPEST • AUCKLAND

ISBN 0-373-12514-3

THE ROYAL BABY BARGAIN

First North American Publication 2006.

Copyright © 2005 by Robyn Kingston.

www.eHarlequin.com

Printed in U.S.A.

HARLEQUIN®
Presents

A warm welcome to all our readers; it's cold outside, but the books Harlequin Presents has got for you in January will leave you positively glowing!

Raise your temperature with two right royal reads! *The Sheikh's Innocent Bride,* by top author Lynne Graham, whisks you away to the blazing dunes of the desert in a classic tale of a proud sheikh's desire for the young woman employed to clean his castle. Meanwhile, Robyn Donald is back with another compelling Bagaton story in *The Royal Baby Bargain,* the latest installment in her immensely popular New Zealand-based BY ROYAL COMMAND miniseries.

Want the thermostat turned up? Then why not travel with us to the glorious Greek islands, where *Bought by the Greek Tycoon,* by favorite author Jacqueline Baird, promises searing emotional scenes and nights of blistering passion, and Susan Stephens's *Virgin for Sale*—the first title in our steamy new miniseries UNCUT—sees an uptight businesswoman learning what it is to feel pleasure in the hands of a *real* man!

For Cathy Williams fans, there's a new winter warmer: in *At the Italian's Command,* the heart of a notoriously cool, workaholic tycoon is finally melted by a frumpy but feisty journalist. And try turning the pages of rising star Melanie Milburne's latest release—*Back in her Husband's Bed,* about a marriage rekindled in sunny Sydney, Australia, is *almost* too hot to handle!

For a full list of titles and book numbers, see inside the front cover (opposite)—and enjoy!

We've captured a slice of royal
life in our miniseries

Kings, counts, dukes and princes…

Don't miss these stories of charismatic kings,
commanding counts, demanding dukes and
playboy princes. Read all about their privileged
lives, love affairs…even their scandals!

Let us treat you like a queen—
relax and enjoy our regal miniseries.

Look out for more stories in this miniseries—
coming in April:
The Royal Marriage
by Fiona Hood-Stewart
#2527

All about the author...
Robyn Donald

Greetings! I'm often asked what made me decide to be a writer of romances. Well, it wasn't so much a decision as an inevitable conclusion. Growing up in a family of readers helped, and shortly after I started school I began whispering stories in the dark to my two sisters. Although most of those tales bore a remarkable resemblance to whatever book I was immersed in, there were times when a new idea would pop into my brain—my first experience of the joy of creativity.

Growing up in New Zealand, in the subtropical north, gave me a taste for romantic landscapes and exotic gardens. But it wasn't until I was in my mid-twenties that I read a Harlequin book and realized that the country I love came alive when populated by strong, tough men and spirited women.

By then I was married and a working mother, but into my busy life I crammed hours of writing; my family has always been hugely supportive. And when I finally plucked up enough courage to send off a manuscript, it was accepted. The only thing I can compare that excitement to is the delight of bearing a child.

Since then it's been a roller-coaster ride of fun and hard work and wonderful letters from fans.

CHAPTER ONE

ABBY stared at the list of things to do before leaving, and let out a long, slow breath, her brows drawing together as another feather of unease ghosted down her spine. Every item had a slash through it, so her unconscious wasn't trying to warn her she'd forgotten something.

It had started—oh, a couple of months ago, at first just a light tug of tension, a sensation as though she'd lost the top layer of skin, that had slowly intensified into a genuinely worrying conviction that she was being watched.

Was this how Gemma's premonitions had felt? Or had she herself finally succumbed to paranoia?

Whatever, she couldn't take any risks.

Driven into action by the nameless fear, she'd resigned from her part-time job at the doctor's surgery and made plans to disappear from the small town hard against New Zealand's Southern Alps—the town that had been her and Michael's refuge for the past three years.

The same creepy sensation tightened her already-taut nerves another notch. She put the list down on the scrubbed wooden table in the kitchen and prowled once more through the cottage, switching lights on and off as she examined each room.

Back in the inconvenient little living room, chilly now that the fire had collapsed into sullen embers, she stopped beside the bag on the sofa that held necessities for tomorrow's journey. Everything else she and Michael owned—clothes, toys, books—was already stuffed into the boot of her elderly car. Not even a scrap of paper hinted at their three years' residence.

Yet that persistent foreboding still nagged at her. All her life she'd loved to lie in bed and listen to the more-pork call, but tonight she shivered at the little owl's haunting, plaintive cry from the patch of bush on the farm next door. And when she caught herself flinching at the soft wail of the wind under the eaves, she dragged in a deep breath and glanced at her watch.

'Stop it right now!' she said sturdily. 'Nothing's going to happen.'

But the crawling, baseless unease had kept her wired and wide-eyed three hours past her normal bedtime. At this rate she wouldn't sleep a wink.

So why not leave now?

Although she'd planned to start early in the morning, Michael would sleep as well in his child seat as he did in bed. He probably wouldn't even wake when she picked him up. No one would see them go, and at this time of night the roads were empty.

The decision made, she moved quickly to collect and pack her night attire and sponge bag and the clothes she'd put out for Michael in the morning. She picked up her handbag, opened it and groped for the car keys.

Only to freeze at a faint sound—the merest scrabble, the sort of sound a small animal might make as it scuttled across the gravel outside.

A typical night noise, nothing to worry about.

Yet she strained to hear, the keys cutting into her palm as her hand clenched around them. Unfortunately her heart thudded so heavily in her ears it blocked out everything but the bleating of a sheep from the next paddock. The maternal, familiar sound should have been reassuring; instead, it held a note of warning.

'Oh, for heaven's sake, stop being so melodramatic,' she muttered, willing her pulse to settle back into a more even rhythm. 'No one cares a bit that you're leaving Nukuroa.'

Very few people would miss her, and if they knew that she'd been driven away from their remote village by a persistent, irrational foreboding they'd think she was going mad. After all, she'd scoffed at Gemma.

But if she was heading for a breakdown, who would look after Michael—?

'No!' she said firmly.

If she were losing her mind, she'd deal with it once she and Michael were safely away.

She yanked the car keys from her handbag, swearing under her breath when she accidentally dislodged an envelope onto the sofa. It gaped open, light from the centre bulb transforming the fine wavy strands of hair inside to a tawny-gold glory.

Abby's lips tightened. She glanced at the dying fire, but before the thought had time to surface she'd pushed the envelope back into her bag and closed the catch on it.

Shivering, she took in three or four deep, grounding breaths. As soon as she got settled again she'd burn that lock of hair. It was a sentimental fetter to a past long dead; her future was devoted to Michael, which was why the miracle of modern hair colouring now dimmed her bright crown to a dull mouse-brown. A further disguise was the way she wore it, scraped back from her face in a pony-tail that straightened the naturally loose, casual waves.

She endured the change, just as she endured the cheap

clothes in unflattering shades that concealed her slender body. She'd even bought spectacles of plain glass, tinted to mute her tilted, almond-shaped eyes and green-gold irises.

Nothing could hide her mouth, wide and full and far too obvious, even when she'd toned it down with lipstick just the wrong colour. In spite of that, and the cleft in her chin, the camouflage worked.

She'd turned being inconspicuous into an art form. Anyone who took a second glance saw a single mother with no clothes sense and no money, working hard to bring up her child, refusing dates, content to lurk on the edge of life. In a year's time no one in Nukuroa would remember her.

If that thought stung, she had only to recall Michael's laughing, open face when he came running towards her each evening in the child-care centre, the warmth of his hug and kiss when she tucked him into bed, his confidence and exuberant enjoyment of life.

Nothing and nobody was more important than Michael.

And if she was going to take him away tonight, she'd better get going!

Keys dangling from her fingers, she lifted the pack and set off for the front door, only to stop, heart hammering again, when her ears picked up the faint murmur of a car on the road. After a second's hesitation, she dropped the pack and paced noiselessly across to the window. Slowly she drew back the curtain a fraction and peered into the darkness. Headlights flashed on and off like alarm beacons in the heavy darkness as the car moved past the line of trees separating the farm paddock from the road.

When the vehicle continued out of sight she let out a long, relieved breath. Her wide mouth sketched a curve at the familiar fusillade of barks from the dogs at the homestead next door, but the smile soon faded. Odd that a car should be on the road this late; in this farming district most people went to bed early.

Taut and wary, she stayed at the window for several more minutes, listening to the encompassing silence, her mind racing over her plans. First the long trip to Christchurch, where she'd sell the car for what little she could get. Tomorrow evening she and Michael would take flight to New Plymouth in the North Island—with tickets bought under a false name, of course.

And then a new safe haven, a different refuge—but the same life, she thought wearily, always checking over her shoulder, waiting for Caelan Bagaton—referred to by the media as Prince Caelan Bagaton, although he didn't use the title—to track her down.

Yet it was a life she'd willingly accepted. Straightening her shoulders, she drew the scanty curtain across and went into the narrow, old-fashioned kitchen, where her gaze fell on the list of things to do. Oh, *hell*! She'd have to get rid of that before she left. Still listening alertly, she screwed up the sheet of paper and dropped it into the waste-paper bin.

Only to give a short, silent laugh at her stupidity, snatch it out and hurry back to the living room to toss it onto the dying embers. It didn't catch immediately; some of the words stood out boldly as the paper curled and blackened, so she bent down and blew hard, and a brief spurt of flame reduced the list to dark flakes that settled anonymously onto the grate.

'Nobody,' she said on a note of steely satisfaction, 'is going to learn anything from those ashes.'

She stood up and had taken one step across the room when she heard another unknown sound. *Where?*

Twanging nerves drove her to move swiftly, noise-lessly, into the narrow hall and head for the door. Two steps away from it, she heard the snick of a key in the lock.

Fear kicked her in the stomach, locking every muscle. For a few, irretrievable seconds she couldn't obey the mindless, adrenalin-charged instinct to snatch up Michael and race wildly out of the back door.

I must be dreaming, she thought desperately. Oh God, please let me be dreaming!

But the door flew back at the noiseless thrust of an impatient hand, and every nightmare that had haunted her sleep, every fear she'd repressed, coalesced into stark panic.

Every magnificent inch an avenging prince, Caelan Bagaton came into the house in a silent, powerful rush, closing the door behind him with a deliberation that dried her mouth and sent her blood racing through her veins. He looked like some dark phantom out of her worst nightmare—tall, broad-shouldered, his hard, handsome features clamped in a mask of arrogant authority. The weak light emphasised the ruthless angle of his jaw and the hard male beauty of his mouth, picked out an auto-cratic sweep of cheekbones and black lashes that con-trasted shockingly with cold blue eyes.

Beneath the panic, a treacherous wildfire memory stirred. Horrified, Abby swallowed. Oh, she remembered that mouth—remembered the feel of it possessing hers…

'You know you should always have a chain on the door,' he said, voice cool with mockery, gaze narrowed and glinting as he scanned her white face.

Shaking but defiantly stubborn, she said, 'Get out,' only to realise that no sound came from her closed throat.

She swallowed and repeated the words in a croaking monotone. 'Get out of here.'

Even though she mightn't be able to master her body's primitive response to his vital potency, she'd stand her ground.

'Did you really think you'd get away with stealing my nephew?' Contempt blazed through every word. He advanced on her, the dominant framework of his face as implacable as the anger that beat against her.

The metallic taste of fear nauseated her; determined not to be intimidated, she fought it with every scrap of will-power. Although she knew it was futile, desperation forced her to try and sidetrack him.

'How did you get the door key?' she demanded, heart banging so noisily she was certain he could hear it.

'I'm the new tenant.' He surveyed her pinched face in a survey as cold as the lethal sheen on a knife-blade. 'And you are Abigail Moore, whose real name is Abigail Metcalfe, shortened by her friends and lovers—and my sister—to Abby.' His tone converted the sentence to an insult. 'Drab clothes and dyed hair are a pathetic attempt at disguise. You must have been desperate to be found.'

'If so, I'd have kept both my hair colour and my name,' she said through her teeth, temper flaring enough to hold the fear at bay.

His wide shoulders lifted in a dismissive shrug. 'Why didn't you move to Australia?'

'Because I couldn't afford the fare.' The words snapped out before she realised she'd been goaded into losing control. Just after she'd returned to New Zealand she'd read an article about him; he'd said that anger and fear made fools of people, and now she was proving it.

Dragging in a shallow breath, she tried again to divert him away from the child sleeping in the back bedroom.

'If you're the new tenant, you're not legally allowed in here until tomorrow. Get out before I call the police.'

He glanced ostentatiously at the sleek silver—no, probably platinum—watch on his lean wrist. 'It is tomorrow, and we both know you won't call the police. The local constable would laugh at you as he tossed you into the cells; kidnappers are despised, especially those who steal babies.'

Panic paralysed her mind until a will-power she hadn't known she possessed forced it into action again; for Michael's sake she had to keep a clear head. She said raggedly, 'I don't know what you're talking about.'

In a drawl as insulting as it was menacing, he said, 'You barely waited to bury Gemma after the cyclone before you stole her child and ran away.'

'We were air-lifted out to New Zealand.' She hid the panicky flutter in her stomach with a snap.

He ignored her feeble riposte with a contemptuous lift of one sable brow. 'I imagine the poor devils on Palaweyo were so busy cleaning up that no one had time or inclination to check any information you gave.' He paused, as though expecting an answer; when she remained stoically silent he finished, 'It was clever—although dangerous—to say he was your child.'

Abby clamped her teeth over more tumbling, desperate words, only will-power keeping her gaze away from the door to Michael's bedroom. Fear coalesced into a cold pool beneath her ribs.

What else did Gemma's brother know?

Claiming Michael as her own might have been illegal, but it had secured his future. Once the prince discovered that his sister had died in one of the Pacific Ocean's violent cyclones, he'd have flown to Palaweyo. And when he found that Gemma had given birth to a child, everything she'd feared—and made Abby promise to prevent—would have unfolded. He'd have taken Michael back to the life that Gemma dreaded—a life of privilege, bereft of love.

Abby's lie had worked a minor miracle; nobody had queried it. Instead, the overworked and pressured island authorities had immediately found her a flight to New Zealand, and once back home the authorities had fast-tracked documentation for her and Michael as mother and child.

She said stonily, 'He is mine.'

'Prove it.'

The words slashed her composure into ribbons. 'Check his birth certificate.' Trying to conceal her fear with a show of defiance, she stared at him with hostile eyes, but her glare backfired into sabotage.

She'd met the prince a few times, usually when she'd called at his opulent mansion in one of Auckland's exclusive marine suburbs to pick up Gemma for an evening out. And once, when she and Gemma were spending a weekend at the beach house on the island he owned in the exquisite Hauraki Gulf, he arrived unexpectedly.

It had been an odd, extremely tense two days; she'd been certain he disliked her, until the final night when he'd kissed her on the beach under the light of a full, voluptuous moon.

She'd gone up in flames, and it had been Caelan who'd pulled away, apologising in a cold, distant voice that had chilled her through to her bones.

Snob, she thought now, compulsively noting the subtle changes the years had made to his arrogant face—a few lines around his cold eyes, a stronger air of authority. His potent charisma still blazed forth, and beneath bronzed skin the splendid bone structure remained rock-hard and ruthless, as it would for the rest of his life.

That ruthlessness was stamped in his family tree. He looked every inch what he was—the descendant of Mediterranean princes who'd established their rule with tough, uncompromising pragmatism and enough hard tenacity to fight off pirates and corsairs and a horde of other invaders, all eager to occupy the rich little island nation of Dacia.

He could have used his social position and his astonishing good looks to lead the life of a playboy. Instead, he'd taken over his father's business in his mid-twenties and used his formidable intellect and intimidating personality to build it into a huge, world-wide organisation.

Add to that power the fact that he kissed like a fallen angel and Abby knew she had every reason to be afraid of the impact he made on her. Praying he couldn't see the mindless, bitter attraction stirring inside her, she wrenched her gaze away.

'I haven't changed as much as you,' he observed silkily. 'But then, I haven't tried to.'

A potent dose of adrenalin pounded through her veins, and, shockingly, for the first time in years she felt alive again.

He noted the heat in her cheeks with a coldly cynical smile. 'The child's birth certificate is a pack of lies,' he said with deadly precision, his hard, beautiful mouth curling.

Her heart contracted. She had to take a deep breath before she could ask, 'Can you prove that?'

'I've seen him.'

She stared at him, eyes huge and dark in her pale face. 'So?'

'He looks like Gemma,' he said flatly. 'I have a photograph of her at the same age, and, apart from the colouring, it looks like the same child.'

'You call that proof?' she asked, letting manufactured scorn ring through her voice. 'You'll need to do better than that to convince anyone.'

Caelan let the silence drag on, ratcheting up her tension until she had to stifle a small gasp when he finally drawled, 'Are you prepared to have a DNA test done?'

It was a trap, of course, and her only chance was to carry it off with a high hand.

'Of course not.' She hoped her contempt matched his.

'I could force you to.'

He meant it. Panic kicked ferociously in her stomach. 'How?'

His mouth thinned into a hard line. 'I have signed depositions from the villagers on Palaweyo—the one where you lived with Gemma—that the boy child was born to the girl with long black hair, not to the nurse who had hair like the sunrise in summer.' He studied her drab hair for a moment of exquisite torture before drawling, 'Any court would take that information as an indication that blood tests would be a good thing.'

The walls in the narrow hall pressed around Abby, robbing her of breath, clamping her heart in intolerable fear. Speared by anguish, she had to concentrate on keeping herself upright. Gemma, she thought numbly, oh Gemma, I'm so sorry...

She could still hear Gemma say, 'And I *won't* go and live with Caelan after the baby's born, so it's no use trying to make me.'

Abby had twisted in the hammock and stared at her very pregnant guest, sprawled out on the coarse white coral sand. 'Don't go all drama queen on me again! I'm not trying to *make* you do anything! All I said was that your brother seems the sort of man who'd be there for you!'

Gemma said with false heartiness, 'Oh, he is! Believe me, they don't come any more protective or autocratic or masterful than Caelan. It's in the genes—all the Bagaton men are tough and dominant. I'm not telling him about this baby because—' She stopped and sifted sand through her fingers, her expression an odd mixture of defiance and shyness. After a swift upwards glance at Abby, she began again. 'Because Caelan would step in and take us over, and for once I want to show him that I can manage.'

Doubtfully, Abby said, 'Gemma, being a single mother isn't easy.' Even when you're cushioned by money and an assured position in world society!

'I can learn. Other women do it,' Gemma said stubbornly.

'Not princesses!'

Gemma grinned. 'We don't use the title—well, not anywhere else but Dacia, where they do it automatically.' The smile faded. 'And don't try to persuade me to let my mother know either. She couldn't care less what I do. As for a grandchild—she'd kill me sooner than own to one! She never loved me, not even as a child. In fact, just before I came to stay with you she told me that she blamed me entirely for the break-up of her marriage to my father!'

'Oh, no, I'm sure she didn't…' But at Gemma's hard little laugh, her voice trailed away.

'Abby, you don't know how much I envy you those parents who loved you, and your normal happy life. I grew up in a huge house that always seemed empty and cold, with parents who fought all the time. In a way it got better after my mother left my father and I was packed off to boarding school and ignored.'

'Even by Caelan?'

Gemma shrugged, one hand stroking her thickening waistline. 'No,' she admitted. 'When he came home it was wonderful, but he was away most of the time, first at university and then overseas.'

'I still can't see why you don't tell him you're pregnant. I know he's tough, and he's obviously been a fairly difficult guardian, but even you admit he did his best for you.'

Gemma pouted. 'Well, that's part of the problem. Caelan has hugely high standards, standards I entirely failed to live up to.'

Talking to Gemma sometimes felt like trying to catch butterflies with your hands behind your back. Abby said gently, 'What's the other part of the problem?'

Gemma gave her a swift, upwards glance, then shrugged elaborately. 'You'll laugh.'

'Try me.'

For once Gemma looked self-conscious. 'Caelan says it's all hokum, but I get—premonitions. I knew when—' in a betraying gesture her hand spread out over her stomach '—when the baby's father went up to rescue those wretched climbers on Mount Everest I knew I'd never see him again. I pleaded with him to stay away, but his damned sense of responsibility drove him there. He saved them, but he died on the mountain himself.'

Abby made a soft, sympathetic noise.

Gemma looked up with tear-drenched eyes and said with sudden, passionate energy, 'OK, it sounds utterly stupid, but I think—I feel—I'm going to die soon after this baby is born.' Ignoring Abby's shocked exclamation, she hurried on, 'If I do, he'll go to live with Caelan and I couldn't bear for him to grow up like me in some huge, formal, echoing house with no parents to love him, no one to hold him when he cries except a nanny who's paid to look after him.'

'Gemma—'

'I know you don't believe me—that's all right. Only—if it happens, Abby, will you take Michael and love him and give him the sort of childhood you had?' She gave a teasing smile, and added, 'If you don't, damn it, I'll haunt you!'

Of course Abby hadn't believed that her guest's premonitions meant anything. She'd set herself to easing what she thought was maternal fear, and felt she'd managed it quite well, but Gemma had been right. Michael had only been two weeks old when one of the Pacific Ocean's vicious cyclones had changed course and smashed into Palaweyo so swiftly there had been no time to evacuate the weather coast.

They'd taken refuge in the hospital, but a beam had fallen on Gemma, breaking her spine. And before she'd died, she'd extracted a promise from Abby—one she was determined to keep.

Whatever it took.

Abby dragged in a deep breath and stared at Caelan's dark, impervious face. Attack, she thought bleakly; don't go all defensive.

'Whatever bribes you paid the villagers—and I hope they were good big ones because they need the money—he's mine.'

'I gave them a new hospital—cyclone-proof this time—and staff to run it.' Caelan's tone was dismissive, but there was nothing casual in his eyes. Icy, merciless, scathing, they raked her face. 'I know the child is Gemma's son.' Watching her with the still intentness of a hunter the moment before he launched a weapon, he finished with charged menace, 'Which makes me his uncle and you no relation at all.'

Abby's head felt woolly and disconnected. Regulating her breath into a slow, steady rhythm, she fought for composure. If the prince knew for certain she was no relation to the child he'd get rid of her so fast that Michael would wake up tomorrow without the only mother he'd ever known.

She loved Michael more than she had ever loved anything else.

Ignoring the cold hollowness inside her, she swallowed to ease her dry throat and said tonelessly, 'Michael is *my* son.'

Caelan hadn't expected to feel anything beyond justified anger and contempt for her, but her dogged stubbornness elicited an unwilling admiration.

Not that she looked anything like the radiant, fey creature who'd met his eyes with a barely hidden challenge four years previously.

In spite of that, in spite of everything she'd done, he still wanted her. He had to clench his hands to stop them from reaching out to her—to shake her? Or kiss the lie from her lips? Both, probably.

The lust should have died the moment he'd discovered she'd stolen Gemma's son.

Deriding himself, he examined her mercilessly, enjoying the colour that flared into her exquisite skin and the wariness shadowing her eyes. Even with bad hair colouring and depressing clothes, her riotous hair confined in brutal subjugation and her eyes hidden behind tinted spectacles, her sensuous allure reached out to him.

Golden as a faerie woman, as dangerous as she was treacherous, behind the almond-shaped eyes and voluptuous mouth hid a lying, scheming kidnapper.

The dossier said that the child seemed happy, but who knew what had happened to Gemma's son?

And why had she done it? Was she one of those sick creatures who yearned so strongly for a child she stole one? One glance at her glittering eyes despatched that idea. She was as sane as he was. So had she thought that possession of Gemma's child would lead to a direct line to Gemma's money?

He changed tactics. 'How much is it going to cost me?'

The last tinge of soft apricot along her astonishing cheekbones vanished, leaving her the colour of parchment. Arms swinging out to catch her, Caelan took an involuntary step forward, then let his hands fall to his sides when she didn't stagger. Sardonically, he watched her eyes close, their long lashes casting fragile shadows on her tender skin.

Oh, she knew all the tricks! He took a deliberate step backwards, removing himself, he thought with cold disgust at his body's betrayal, from danger.

Her lashes lifted and she transfixed him with eyes that usually blended green and gold; not now, though. Stripped of all emotion, enamelled and opaque, they blazed a clear, hard green, vivid in the dim light of the small, bare hall.

'How much for what?' she asked in a staccato sentence.

He didn't bother with subtlety. 'For you to give up the child.'

CHAPTER TWO

NOT a muscle moved in the delicate ivory skin, but a shadow darkened Abby's eyes. 'You disgust me,' she said woodenly. 'Get out.'

Time, Caelan decided, to use the blunt instrument; if appealing to greed wouldn't do the trick, threats usually worked. 'You're in trouble, Abby. If I decide to play it heavy, you face a conviction for kidnapping the child and giving false information to the passport authorities.'

That shocked her. She winced as though against a blow, but her soft mouth hardened. 'His name is *Michael*,' she stated fiercely, shaken by a gust of emotion he couldn't define. 'He's not some entity you can define by the term *child*; he has a personality, a place in the world.'

'A place in the world?' Caelan looked around the shabby hall, his derision plain. 'He deserves better than this.'

'*You* might have grown up in the lap of luxury, secure in the fact that you're a prince, but most children are perfectly happy with a more down-market set of relatives and much less money. He is loved and he loves. He has little friends—'

'You're taking him away from them,' he interrupted in his turn, not trying to hide the contempt in his tone.

She looked away. Whatever she'd been going to say died on her tongue; she shivered, and once more delicate colour flared along her high cheekbones. On a burst of fierce, angry triumph, Caelan knew that he wasn't the only one feeling the violent pull of an old craving.

'Let's deal,' he said, forcing himself to speak judicially. Clearly, she wasn't going to be bought off, so he had no choice; she was the only mother Gemma's son had known, and, until the child could manage without her, they were both stuck with her.

Not that he was going to tell her that. No, he'd frighten her thoroughly first, and then drive as hard a bargain as he could.

With cool deliberation, he went on, 'I'm offering you a future. I want the—I want my sister's child. However, because he thinks you're his mother, I propose we bury the hatchet.'

Torn by a tumult of conflicting thoughts, she stared at him. 'How?' she said at last, her voice stiff and defensive, waiting for his next words with painful apprehension.

He said ironically, 'It's quite simple.'

'Simple?' Abby was so incensed she almost gobbled the word. 'Nothing about this is simple.'

'You should have thought of that before you decided to play with Michael's life,' the prince said grimly. 'You removed him from his family, took him away from the only people who'd know how to protect him. Have you thought of the danger you could be exposing him to?'

'Danger?' Eyes widening, she stared at him. 'What danger?'

He said coldly, 'He's a Bagaton, which makes him prime kidnap material.'

So shocked she almost fell for the trick, she had to bite back the words that trembled on her lips. Hoping he didn't notice the momentary hesitation, she said haughtily, 'He is not a Bagaton. His name is Michael Metcalfe.

And we Metcalfes are noted for our long and happy marriages, not for being kidnapped.'

A slashing jet brow rose in irony. 'A writer is sniffing around Palaweyo, researching a book on Pacific tragedies.' His hard, sensuous mouth curled. 'Any woman you can label a princess is always useful when it comes to selling books, especially if she's young and beautiful and dies in a monster cyclone after giving birth. Once the writer finds out that Michael is Gemma's child—'

Abby struggled to remain calm, but the panic beneath her ribs intensified so that she couldn't control her racing thoughts. 'I doubt whether any writer—however well his books sell!—can afford to dangle the bribe of a hospital in front of the villagers in return for the right lies,' she flashed.

'I knew that the child was Gemma's before I decided to give the villagers their hospital,' he told her casually. 'They spoke quite freely about you and her—they have no reason not to tell anyone who asks. And no writer worth his salt is going to keep it quiet.' His face hardened. 'Inevitably you will be tracked down—'

'How? It took you, with all your resources, three years to find us,' she snapped, but he could see the fear in her eyes.

'Writers have resources too.' He waited while she absorbed the impact of that before adding forcefully, 'Once he finds you, the resultant publicity will expose Michael's existence—and his lack of protection—to anyone who wants a quick fortune. Didn't you read about the de Courcy heiress?'

Colour drained from Abby's face. The fourteen-year-old daughter of a billionaire had been snatched from her exclusive school, yet although her parents had paid the huge ransom, it had been too late. She'd been killed the day after she'd disappeared.

The cold, inflexible voice of the prince battered at her composure. 'Whoever did that got away with five million euros, worth in New Zealand dollars about—'

'I know how much it's worth! You're trying to frighten me,' she said thinly, turning her head away from his intimidating gaze as though she could shut out the effect of his words.

'Damn right I am! There are people out there who'd see Michael as a passport to easy money, a soft target. Are you willing to risk that?'

She went even paler and closed her eyes. He was manipulating her, but the thought of Michael in the clutches of some cold-hearted psychopath robbed her of speech and the ability to think.

A soft noise brought her head around sharply; Michael was stirring. And the prince was walking with long, noiseless strides towards the open door of the bedroom.

Panic hit her in a howling, destructive storm, propelling her after him into the tiny room. Caelan loomed over the bed. He didn't move, didn't acknowledge her presence at all, his whole attention bent on the child as though claiming him in some primal way.

Abby pushed desperately at his hard, lean body. She might as well have tried to move a granite pillar, except that his body heat reached out and blasted through the brittle shell of her self-control.

Her hands dropped, but she didn't move. In a fierce voice pitched too low to disturb the restless child, she ordered, 'Get out of here.'

Silently Caelan turned, but he waited at the doorway, a silent, threatening figure. After straightening the bedclothes over Michael, Abby dragged in a juddering breath and left him.

'We'll go into the living room.' She pushed open the door.

Once inside Caelan Bagaton said with cold distaste, 'I don't hurt children, Abby.'

'All right, I overreacted,' she returned shakily. 'I don't think you'd be cruel to him. I know you weren't cruel to Gemma—she told me herself that she barely knew you because you were away so much. But can't you see that the last thing she wanted was for her son to be banished to a nursery like an abandoned doll stuffed in a cupboard, cared for by nannies who come and go regularly?'

Caelan's expression didn't change at her inadvertent admission that the child was Gemma's. His desire to see the boy had shattered Abby's composure; she didn't even realise she'd given herself away.

Instinct warned him to proceed with caution. He said neutrally, 'Her mother wasn't maternal, but she made sure Gemma had the best care available. And my father had duties he couldn't avoid, as well as a corporation to run. He did his best for her.'

Hands clenching into fists at her side, Abby skewered him with an outraged glance and carried on in full, indignant fervour. 'By sending her off to boarding school the minute she turned eight, where she was wretchedly, miserably unhappy? That was his *best*?' With an elaborate dismissive shrug she finished scathingly, 'In that case, I'm really, really glad to hear that he didn't dislike her!'

'That's enough!'

Caelan's harsh, deep voice drowned her in cold menace. Damn, she thought, mortified; don't let emotion get the better of you! She could see contempt in his eyes, in the hard line of his mouth, the still tautness of his powerful body. No matter how angry he was, the prince remained in full control.

'Admit that he's Gemma's child.' At her obstinate silence, he said coolly, 'You asked for proof that he's not yours. Here it is.'

He drew a sheet of paper from the pocket of his casual, superbly cut jacket. When he offered it to her she took it and tried to read, but the words danced and blurred in front of her eyes. Blinking, she forced her brain to focus.

Couched in scientist's prose, it was quite definite; there were enough points of similarity between tissue samples one and two for there to be a familial connection.

'I don't understand,' she whispered, fighting off dark dread. The paper dropped from her nerveless fingers.

Watching her with unsparing eyes, the prince made no attempt to pick it up.

When she regained enough composure to be able to speak again, she said stiffly, 'This could be anyone's samples. There's no way you could take a blood sample from Michael without my knowing, and I know you didn't get one from me.'

His beautiful mouth relaxed into a sardonic smile. 'Blood isn't necessary for DNA testing—any tissue will serve.' His inflexible tone warned her. Heart hammering, she listened as he went on. 'And I didn't need one from you. It was easy enough to send in a worker at the childcare centre; she stayed three weeks before deciding she didn't like living in the backblocks, and she came away with saliva samples and blood from a grazed knee. The results prove that you're not Michael's mother—that you're no relation to him.'

Blood roared through her head as outrage manhandled fear aside. She grabbed the back of the sofa and fought for control, finally grinding out, 'How dare you? You had no right to—'

'You had no *right* to steal my sister's child,' he cut in, his lethal tone quelling her anger as effectively as a douche of ice water. 'Why did you do it? What satisfaction did it give you?'

'Gemma asked me to take care of him.'

The strong bone structure of his face was very much in evidence. Dispassionately he said, 'If she did, it was typically dramatic and thoughtless of her to demand that you put your life on hold for Michael, but that's irrelevant now.' He paused, his hooded eyes keen and watchful. 'The next step is a court case, where the first thing any judge will do is order another DNA test. And we both know how that will turn out.'

An acceptance of defeat rose like bitter anguish inside Abby. She was going to lose Michael. But not, she thought grimly, until she'd made this arrogant prince fight to the last for his nephew.

Pride and disillusion gave her voice an acid edge when she said, 'If all you're planning for Michael is a lonely, loveless childhood like Gemma's, why on earth do you want him?'

'Because he is a Bagaton,' he said coldly.

'Gemma was a Bagaton too, but it didn't make her happy. She wanted me to look after him.' When he raised his brows she cried, 'I've got a letter to prove it.'

She stooped to her bag, holding her shoulders stiffly and her spine so rigid she thought it might splinter. With trembling fingers she unzipped an inner pocket in one suitcase and took out an envelope.

Thrusting it at the man who watched her with eyes as translucent and cold as polar ice, she said, 'Here.'

He took it, but didn't look at it. His startlingly good-

looking face was set in lines of such formidable determination that she flinched, yet a melting heat in the pit
of her stomach astonished and frightened her. It was one
thing to acknowledge that he had a primitive physical
power over her; it would be shameful to let her body's
treachery weaken her.

'Read it,' she said desperately. 'It will make any judge
think about his decision.'

Frowning, the prince examined the single sheet of
notepaper.

Abby waited tensely, mentally going over the words
she knew by heart.

Dearest Abby, If you're reading this I'm dead. See,
I told you I could foretell things! Take Michael to New
Zealand, but make sure neither Caelan nor my mother
find you—or him. I know you love my baby, and I
know you'll take care of him. And thanks for being
my wise, sensible friend. Don't grieve too much. Just
keep on loving Michael, and look after him.

In a voice without the slightest trace of emotion,
Caelan said, 'It certainly looks as though Gemma wrote
it—I recognise the aura of drama and doom.' His long
fingers tightened on the sheet of paper and he looked at
her from half-closed eyes, his mouth twisting. 'You're
too trusting, Abby. What's to stop me tearing it to shreds
and lying about seeing it?'

Oddly enough, it hadn't occurred to her. His reputation
for fair dealing matched the one for ruthlessness. Her
mouth tightened. 'It's a copy; the real one is in a solicitor's office,' she said steadily.

The hard, uncompromising determination stamped on

Caelan's lean, bronze face was replaced by a gleam of humour.

Her susceptible heart missed a beat. Although Gemma had told her that he despised people who used their charm to dazzle others, he possessed an inordinate amount of it himself. His smile was a weapon, a dangerously disturbing challenge that had penetrated stronger defences than hers.

Lazily he said, 'I'd have been disappointed if you hadn't made sure of that. But this means nothing; I can produce evidence to show that Gemma was a fragile, emotionally unstable woman, incapable of knowing what was best for her child.'

Abby opened her mouth, but honesty stopped the fierce words that threatened to spill out. Yes, Gemma had been fragile, as well as funny and delightful, but she'd been absolutely determined Michael wouldn't grow up without love and attention.

Caelan looked around the small room furnished with cheap, shabby cast-offs. The harsh central light turned Abby's skin sallow and robbed her hair of highlights or any depth of colour. It was, he thought with cool cynicism, a sin to hide that glorious mane of red-gold hair.

And an even greater one to cover her slender body with a loose black T-shirt and pair of dust-coloured corduroy trousers.

He banished tantalising memories of the figure beneath the shapeless clothes, sleek and lithe and strong, her exquisite skin an instant temptation...

And her mouth, soft and hot and delicious beneath his, opening to him with an eagerness that still affected him.

Abby had strayed into his life, a glowing, sensuous girl who seemed unaware of her sexual power. Not that he believed in her innocence; Gemma chose friends who tended to be sophisticated and spoilt.

Already in a very satisfying relationship with another woman, he'd put Abby resolutely from his mind. Yet he hadn't been able to prevent himself from kissing her—a kiss that had led directly to the termination of his affair. And when Gemma told him the fey, strangely tempting health worker had gone to some backwater Pacific island for a year on a volunteer basis, he'd been taken aback by an odd sense of loss.

Then all hell had broken loose in a far-flung part of the business; he'd spent months unravelling the mess while Gemma had stayed with her mother in Australia. Caelan didn't like his stepmother, but he kept in touch with his sister, and when she'd written to say she was on Palaweyo spending time with Abby, he'd decided to call in and re-acquaint himself with the alabaster-skinned girl, discover if the provocation in her inviting mouth and tilted eyes was genuine or a cynical come-on.

But the cyclone had intervened, and by the time he'd got to Palaweyo, Gemma was dead and buried and Abby had vanished with her child.

Abby swung to face him, her movements graceful in spite of her tension. 'Do you honestly believe Michael might be in danger?'

'It's always a possibility,' he said, but she broke in, colour returning in a soft flood to her skin with the heat of her response.

'I want the truth.' She paused, searching for words, then forced herself to say unevenly, 'I know that someone in your position might be seen as a target, but Michael has nothing.'

He said ironically, 'He has a very rich uncle and a large trust fund.'

Stunned, she stared at him, realising the implications of this. No wonder he was suspicious—did he believe she had her eye on that rich trust fund? 'I didn't know,' she said, knowing he wouldn't believe her.

He gave her a look that should have frozen the words on her lips. 'Come on, Abby! I'm sure Gemma spent a lot of time complaining about the cruel brother who kept such a tight grip on the purse strings, but you knew she didn't have to work.'

'I thought—I thought you made her an allowance.'

Looking down the arrogant blade of his nose, he said with forbidding restraint, 'My father made sure she was provided for.'

If anything had been needed to point up the difference between them, his casual words did it. In the prince's world children were set up with trust funds, whereas Abby had grown up on an orchard. Although her parents had worked hard, when they'd died they'd left little for her—just enough for her to pay her way for a year on Palaweyo to help the community with their health needs.

He said forcefully, 'I didn't approve of the way Gemma was relegated to the outer perimeter of her mother's life. It won't happen with her son.' His tone edged each word with satire. 'I don't intend sending Michael to boarding school until he reaches secondary school. Not even then, if he doesn't want it.' He directed an ice-laden glance around the bleak room. 'He'll be much better off with me than with a woman who's both a kidnapper and a liar, and who lives from hand to mouth in a rural slum.'

Abby forced back the bubble of hysteria that threatened to block her throat and her thought processes. 'At least I love him!'

Dark brows lifted in taunting disbelief. 'It's an odd

love that confines a child to a life in places like this. And this isn't about you or me—this is about Michael, whose rights should be paramount. After all, it's *his* future that's on the line.'

'He has all the security he needs,' she retorted, trying hard to sound sensible and confident—and failing. The thought of Michael's life at the hands of this flinty, uncompromising tyrant edged her tone with desperation. 'What can *you* offer him? I'm sure that chasing yet another million to add to the pile you've already accumulated will take precedence over spending time with a little boy.'

His white teeth snapped together. After a taut few seconds he returned caustically, 'At least he won't have to worry where his next meal is coming from.'

'He's never gone hungry.' Occasionally she had, but not Michael. 'What do you know about children? He's noisy and grubby and demanding, and he needs attention and love and the knowledge that he's hugely important to at least one person in this world. Even more, he needs to know that that person will be there whenever he wants her, not just for an hour after work. All your money and royal links and social position mean *nothing* compared to that.'

'So why did you send him to a child-care centre with constantly changing workers, most of them almost untrained?'

Goaded, she retorted, 'I needed the money, and it was only for half of each day.'

He shrugged dismissively, the swift movement reminding her of his Latin heritage. 'A nanny would provide more stability, and I can certainly make sure he never has to worry about feeling cold in winter.'

Abby stared at him, defiance crumbling under guilt and

fear. She took refuge in sarcasm. 'Of course, you know so much about small boys.'

'I was one once.'

She snorted. 'I don't believe that. You were born six feet four tall and breathing fire.'

Amazingly, his hard mouth quirked. 'If so, my mother never told me.' The momentary amusement disappeared instantly, replaced by chilling hauteur. 'Stop fencing. I asked you before—how much do you want to get out of his life?'

'And I told you that I won't sell him,' she retorted furiously.

A faint stain of colour along his high, magnificent cheekbones told her she'd hit a nerve. The raw note in his voice hardened into intimidating confidence. 'I'm not buying the child—I'm buying *you* off.'

His narrowed gaze sent shivers of sensation along every nerve in her body. Her breath stopped in her throat, and something stark and merciless and fierce linked them for a charged moment, until she saw the glint of satisfaction in his cold eyes.

He knew, she thought in wretched embarrassment. Of course he did—he'd been chased by women since his teens; what he knew about them would probably fill an encyclopaedia. He certainly realised her treacherous body had its own agenda, and it amused him to see her struggle against it.

Abby took an involuntary step backwards—a mistake, she realised instantly, and tried to cover it with a swift, proud retort. 'You don't have enough money—no one in the whole wide world has enough money—to buy Michael from me, so forget about it right now.'

His broad shoulders moved in a slight shrug that told her just how much this meant to him: nothing. 'Judging by all accounts you have done a good job with the boy. I'm offering some recompense.'

She stated, 'I'm not going to abandon him to a loveless life.' And wished she'd put it some other way because it sounded so prissy.

'I intend to love him.' His tone was glacial, as though she'd forced some shameful secret from him.

She said urgently, 'You can't fake emotion. It doesn't work like that. You, of all people, should know. Gemma said that you and she had been taught in a hard school that love is a weakness.'

'Trust Gemma to pile on the melodrama. Yes, my father was notoriously besotted with his second wife, and losing her to another man shattered him. That doesn't mean that I don't know how to love a child.'

Abby made a swift, rapidly controlled gesture, then froze as the quiet hum of an expensive engine broke into the tense silence.

The prince said crisply, 'It's a hire car. I'm going to the airport in Queenstown and my nephew is coming with me. Try to stop me, and I'll call the police.'

His tone—level, impervious, relentless—echoed in the silent room. The car drew up outside the house and the driver switched off the engine, although Abby could see the round circles of the headlights through the curtains.

Bitter pain stopped any words from escaping her lips. Wringing her hands together in futile agony, she could only look pleadingly at Caelan's inflexible face.

He glanced down at the sheet of paper in his hands and appeared to come to some decision. 'All right. I believe that it would be exceedingly bad to put him through the trauma of waking up and finding you gone.' He lifted his head to pin her with cool detachment. 'You can come with us, but on my terms.'

Elusive, defiant hope flickered like a candle in a draught. Tautly she demanded, 'Which are?'

'That you accept I've got a right to know my nephew.'

Too afraid to be cautious, she accepted bitter defeat. 'I—yes.' Indeed, it had always worried her that Michael was being deprived of what was left of his family.

Caelan nodded. 'We can negotiate everything else when you're a little less emotional,' he said, his mouth compressing into a straight line. When she didn't answer or move he said, 'Make up your mind, Abby. Are you coming with me, or staying here?'

CHAPTER THREE

NUMBLY Abby stared at Caelan, reading his ruthless will in his face, in the uncompromising authority of his tone. Anger was defeated by desolation; she didn't dare trust him, but what other choice did she have?

Impatiently the prince broke into her racing thoughts. 'I'm offering you a chance to stay in Michael's life. Turn it down and I won't give you another.'

'You can't do that,' she croaked. 'I've looked after him since he was a baby. Any court in New Zealand would grant me custody—'

'It is a remote possibility,' he conceded crisply. 'But would the justice system also protect him from any criminal who might see him as money in the bank?'

He paused to let that sink in. Her powerlessness burned like fire inside her, eating away at her will-power and courage. 'I can't believe that that sort of thing would happen here.'

'He won't always be in New Zealand. I have to travel; he'll come with me.'

'But—'

'I thought you despised my father for allowing Gemma to be banished to her nursery?'

Pain sliced through her. 'I—yes.'

With cool dispassion, Caelan inclined his black head. 'The simplest way to deal with this is for you both to come to live with me.'

Stunned, unable to believe that she'd heard him correctly, she stared at him. 'I don't want to live with you and I'm certain you don't want me anywhere around you.'

'True, but I'm a pragmatic man.' His voice was textured by unfaltering confidence. 'It's not negotiable, Abby. That is, if you want to be with Michael.'

Pride brought up her chin, veiled her eyes with thick lashes to hide the bleak shock of his blunt statement. Fighting to salvage what she could from her surrender, she said, 'We don't need to share a house. We—Michael and I—could live in Auckland, and I wouldn't deny you access to him. Michael needs a man in his life.'

The prince surveyed her with a narrow smile. 'How do I know you won't pack your bags and sneak off?'

'If I gave you my word—'

'Why should I trust you?'

The words rang in her ears like iron on stone, cold and hard and relentless. Thrusting his hands into his trouser pockets he sauntered over to the window and looked out at the night. Against the pale luminosity of starshine he was a lean, dominant silhouette.

Abby dragged in a slow, difficult breath, aching with a sense of loss, of defeat and pain, with the knowledge of wasted years that were gone for ever and a future that would never happen. She had no other choice; losing Michael would tear her heart to shreds, and for his sake she had to endure whatever this cold, judgmental aristocrat decided to dish out.

Over his shoulder, he said, 'You've got ten seconds to make up your mind.'

Anger revived her, giving her a spurious energy that helped her say woodenly, 'It won't work.'

'Don't look at me with those huge, horrified eyes,' he said, his negligent tone as much an insult as his careless survey of her. 'You'll be quite safe.'

Colour burned up through her skin. He thought she was afraid for her virtue, and his tone made it clear that she didn't attract him in the least. Humiliated, she snapped, 'I suppose if we move into your house you'll insist on a nanny, and after Michael's got accustomed to her you'll force me to leave.'

'You sound like an actor in a Victorian melodrama. There won't be a nanny unless you want one.' Mockery laced his voice as he turned and examined her, his smile as lethal as a sword-blade. When she remained silent he added, 'I assume you do want the best for Michael?'

'You know I do,' she whispered, frightened by the forbidden excitement that gripped her. 'But not if it means living in the same house as you.'

He shrugged negligently, obviously not in the least affected by her swift, harsh rejection. 'But you'll do it— for his sake.' He watched her white face with cruel detachment. 'We'll make it legal with a cast-iron contract, and if you behave yourself and concentrate on Michael's welfare, there'll even be a cut-off date—say, when he finishes secondary education. In return I'll pay an allowance that will keep you in clothes that suit you and let you grow out your hair. Dying it must have been the ultimate sacrifice.'

'It didn't worry me in the least,' she said flatly.

Clearly he didn't believe her, because her words produced another cold, enigmatic smile. 'Hard to believe, Abby. And you might as well take off those spectacles too. I know they're not necessary.'

Slowly Abby removed the rimless frames, blinking as the light burned into her eyes. She felt stripped of everything she'd tried to hide, nakedly exposed to Caelan Bagaton's hard, penetrating gaze.

He said tersely, 'Gemma might have been right when

she told you that I don't do love well, but I do understand how to protect my own. Although I failed to save Gemma, I can make sure that her son doesn't die before his time.'

Abby hesitated, but something about his tone in the final sentence made her say with quiet intensity, 'No one could have saved Gemma, not even you. The cyclone wasn't supposed to come anywhere near Palaweyo, but at the last moment it turned and roared down on us out of a cloudless sky. We didn't have time to get out—in fact, we only just had time to gather everyone in the hospital. Gemma wouldn't want you to feel that you'd failed her.'

'She died before her time; that sounds like failure to me. So what's your decision?' His voice was icily detached. 'I don't intend to spend all night in this cold, musty room while you dither. Either accept my terms and live in my house with Michael, or forget about him and get on with your life.'

In an agony of indecision, Abby bit her lip. Chilly air seeped across her skin, and the soft noises of the old cottage settling down for the night, usually familiar and comforting, had become tinged with menace.

With the prince's harsh words echoing in her ears, she accepted she had no choice. While surrender was bitter, accepting his ultimatum would afford Michael more security than she could ever offer him.

From behind her Caelan said in a voice edged with cynicism, 'After all, it's a win/win situation. I get my nephew. Michael will be with the only mother he knows. And you can emerge from the melodramatic shadows you've been skulking in, wash the dye out of your hair and buy a whole new wardrobe in the right colours. The Abby I remember dressed to play up her hair and eyes and skin, but the outfit you're wearing now makes you look as though you've got acute jaundice.'

That stung, even though her clothes had been carefully selected to strip the colour from her skin. Bought from the cheapest racks, they couldn't have been more different from the tailored trousers that showed off Caelan's long, heavily muscled legs, or the jersey he wore, its lustrous shine revealing that it was made from merino wool.

'And what's in it for you?' she asked bluntly.

He gave her an ironic glance. 'The knowledge that my nephew isn't hungry and has the position and all the advantages he deserves. Most of all, the knowledge that he's safe.'

Nothing about love there! According to Gemma and the newspapers, Caelan was the consummate sophisticate; he'd soon get bored with the antics of a three-year-old.

Her heart clenched painfully. Even if he couldn't be the sort of father a child needed, she'd be there to provide love and understanding for Michael, and to fight for him whenever it became necessary.

Yet self-protection forced her to search for a less dangerous compromise. 'I still think it would be easier for us all if Michael and I had our own place. You could see him whenever you want to.'

But even as she said the words she knew they weren't going to change Caelan's mind.

'You'll live with me, so I can keep a close watch on you. From now on, wherever Michael goes, either I—or someone I employ—will be half a step behind.' He spoke with the cold, raw impact of a punch in the face, his tone implacable.

'All right,' she said at last, the acrid taste of defeat in

her mouth. She had no room to manoeuvre, and he knew it. Apprehension shivered through her, setting her nerves jumping.

'Then let's go,' he said without expression. 'Do you want me to carry the child out to the car?'

'No,' she said too quickly.

Ignoring her, he strode out of the room and opened the front door, giving crisp, low-voiced orders to whoever had driven the car up to the cottage.

Abby walked back into Michael's room, but once there she fixed her gaze painfully on his beloved face. Even when Caelan came back in she didn't move.

He interrupted her darting thoughts with an impatient command. 'Forget the past—it's not relevant—and think of Michael's well-being; at the moment he needs both of us—me for the security which, believe it or not, Gemma would have considered to be just as important as the love you dispense.' After a tense pause he drawled, 'Or is it too big a sacrifice for you to make for him?'

'Damn you,' she whispered, torn on the rack of her ambivalence, disillusion and pain warring with the ig-nominy of her own helplessness.

A sobbing sigh from the bed broke the thick web of tension between them. Nerves taut and brittle as spun toffee, she sat down on the edge when Michael rubbed his eyes and began to hiccup.

'Hush, darling, it's all right,' she crooned, lifting his solid, warm body against her. 'Did you have a bad dream?'

He murmured something and clung, cuddling into her, so utterly dear that her heart clenched in a tight, hard ball.

Abby kissed his tousled hair and pressed her cheek against it, looking across to where Caelan stood.

Michael must have sensed that someone else was in the room too; he turned his head, his eyes growing larger as he examined Caelan. Sobs dying, he said, 'Abby?'

'Hello, Michael, I'm your Uncle Caelan, and you're coming to live with me.' Caelan's voice was deep and cool and utterly confident.

His nephew stared at him, clutching Abby tighter. 'And Abby too?' he said uncertainly.

Caelan looked at Abby. 'Tell him,' he commanded.

She dragged in a deep breath, praying fiercely that this was the right thing for Michael. 'Of course, darling,' she said simply. 'You know I'll always be with you.'

Michael looked up at her, brows drawing together in a frown that reminded her eerily of the man with them.

'Give him to me,' Caelan ordered.

When she hesitated, he said curtly, 'I'm not a monster, Abby.'

But she handed Michael over with huge reluctance. Carrying the small boy easily, his uncle strode out of the room; swiftly Abby scooped up blankets and Michael's stuffed elephant and the fire engine she'd made of wooden blocks and followed, panting slightly by the time she reached the big, waiting car.

Caelan was stooping, his voice level and reassuring as he lowered Michael into a child seat in the back. Another man stood some distance away—possibly the one who'd kept her under surveillance. A sudden shiver of foreboding tightened her skin.

She didn't understand power at all, whereas Caelan Bagaton reeked of it. Very little of that inherent authority came from the title he rarely used and his heritage; if he'd been born plain Caelan Smith he'd have made his way in the world. He was a winner.

As soon as the restraints on the car seat were clipped

home Michael peered anxiously at Abby, who hovered in the crisp air.

'Sit beside him,' Caelan ordered, straightening up so that she could drape the blankets around the child. 'Give me your car keys first—'

'Why?'

'I assume the bag on the sofa isn't the sum total of your belongings?'

'No, but—'

He frowned, explaining with surprising patience, 'We'll transfer the rest of your luggage from your car to this one. Then someone will drive yours to Auckland.'

Feeling foolish, she muttered, 'I was going to sell it in Christchurch,' and rooted for the keys in her bag. She dropped them into his outstretched hand, noting that he wasn't looking at her; his gaze was fixed on Michael.

She took Michael's warm little hand and coaxed, 'Go back to sleep, darling.'

Caelan stepped back and turned away. As she got in beside Michael and tucked the blankets around him more securely she was aware of the prince's deep voice giving concise orders. The boot was opened, the bags put in and it slammed shut again, before the silence was punctuated by the sound of her car door closing. Its engine coughed into life and headlights probed the darkness as it turned down the drive in front of them.

Caelan slid in behind the wheel of the hire car. Turning so that he could see her, he said negligently, 'Try to stay awake until we get to Queenstown. You can sleep on the plane; there's a bed in it as well as a cot for Michael.'

In the dark cocoon that was the interior of the car she thought his eyes lingered on her face for a second before he turned back and the engine purred into life.

Hot blood stung her skin. What had she done, letting

herself be ambushed and captured like this? The prince took no prisoners; what did he have in mind for her?

A tiredness more than physical, a weariness of the spirit, chilled her from the bones out. While Michael slid back into the sleep of the very young and secure, she stayed wide-eyed and tense until the luxurious car drove into the airport at Queenstown.

But he didn't drive towards the darkened terminal building. 'Where are we going?' she asked.

'There's a private plane waiting on the runway.'

Well, of course, she thought wearily. As well as being cousin to the ruler of a principality, Caelan Bagaton was a tycoon, a billionaire, rich enough to afford his own country as well as a private jet.

Oh, you fool, she thought painfully, you're so far out of your depth here you might as well drown now and get it over and done with.

They'd met when Gemma had almost run her over in one of Auckland's summer storms, and, although her car was a miracle of design that Abby knew she'd never be able to aspire to, Gemma had insisted on taking her home.

Their friendship had ripened rapidly; they'd gone clubbing together and spent other nights talking and listening to music; Gemma had invited her up to the beach house, although she had said, 'But Caelan won't be there.'

Abby's brows shot up. 'So?'

'Oh, just that quite a few of the girls I know try to use me to get to him. And even my friends fall in love with him and then get their hearts broken. He's a big, bad wolf, my brother.'

Well, he'd turned up at the beach, and Abby had found out for herself the truth of that assessment! Fortunately her year abroad working for a volunteer organisation was due to start the week after, so she hadn't had time to brood about Gemma's fabulous, arrogant, incredibly sexy brother.

When she'd left for the Pacific Gemma had wept a little and promised to visit. Abby hadn't expected her to; Palaweyo was a poor atoll, only the bounty of its huge lagoon saving it from third-world status, and few tourists came within a thousand miles. But months later Gemma had arrived, tense and oddly desperate, and during the long hot nights she'd confided a few details of her passionate affair with a gangly, laconic Australian mountainclimber, and his heroic death. Before she'd had time to grieve, she'd discovered that she was pregnant.

Eerily, as though he could read her thoughts, Caelan said, 'I believe Michael's father was another Michael— Moncrieff, the mountaineer who died rescuing stranded climbers on Mount Everest.'

Stunned, Abby swallowed. 'Yes,' she said thinly.

'A decent man, but not her usual sort. Didn't it occur to you that his relatives might have wanted to have contact with their grandchild?'

'Gemma said he had none; he'd grown up in care.'

Something about Caelan's nod made her realise that he knew this. Of course he'd have had Gemma's lover investigated. Suddenly loathing him and everything he stood for, she finished curtly, 'Gemma said he was genuine gold all through.'

Surprisingly Caelan didn't dig further. 'Why does Michael call you Abby? It would have been less obvious if he'd called you his mother.'

'But I'm not his mother,' she said quietly. 'He knows his parents are dead. He doesn't know what that means, of course, but he's entitled to know who he is.'

'But not about his mother's family.'

The lash of his sarcasm flicked across her skin like a whip; she was glad when he eased the car to a stop beside the sleek executive plane.

Once in the aircraft, with Michael asleep in the luxurious bedroom, and the prince going through papers in a leather-upholstered armchair that somehow didn't look incongruous with a seat belt, Abby stared through a window until the sky began to turn grey towards the east. Thoughts churned in her mind, going over and over old ground while she tried to work out how she could have avoided this.

In the end she gave up; against the prince's iron-clad determination she had no defence.

The stark volcanic landscape of the central North Island unrolled beneath the plane as the sun tinted the distant clouds a radiant pink that swiftly turned to gold.

Foolish to let an everyday miracle lift her heart, yet she wondered if the sunrise was some sort of omen, a pointer of hope. Perhaps she and the prince could work together for Michael's sake; perhaps Caelan could find it in his cold heart to learn to love a small child.

And perhaps not, she thought grimly, but staying with Michael was all she asked at the moment.

As though her thoughts had woken him, she saw Michael peep cautiously through the door of the bedroom. He beamed at her before turning to examine his uncle.

Caelan had noticed, of course; he put his papers down and said, 'Good morning, Michael.'

For a moment Michael looked apprehensive, but he was a friendly child and he essayed a tentative grin. Abby's breath locked in her throat; she watched the formidable assurance of Caelan's expression relax into a rare, compelling smile.

Deep inside her something twisted, and a pang of excitement—hot and feverish and piercing—seized her so fiercely she almost gasped under its impact.

'Do you want to go to the bathroom?' his uncle asked.

Michael thought for a moment, then nodded. 'Yes. With Abby.'

'Of course.' An ice-blue, enigmatic gaze roamed Abby's face. 'When you've finished, breakfast will be ready.'

Eyes wide and incredulous, Michael stared around the plane and demanded, 'Where are we, Abby?'

'We're in an aeroplane, darling, up in the sky.' Warily conscious of Caelan's presence, Abby tried to resurrect her brisk common sense. 'When you've been to the bathroom you can look out of the window and you'll see the sea a long way underneath us.'

Bubbling with excitement, Michael shot questions at her on the way to the bathroom and all the way back, falling silent only when he at last saw the sea, a gleaming bow against the craggy bulk of the land.

Caelan said, 'Everything you packed into your car is on the plane; I thought it best for him to have as many familiar things around him as possible.'

'Thank you,' she said in a stilted voice.

'It was nothing.'

And indeed, for him, it wasn't. All he had to do was command, and people hurried to do his bidding. Travelling with the prince was nothing like the normal hassle; leg-room wasn't a problem and luggage didn't need to be monitored. Money made things easy in so many ways, and of course his heritage meant that he took such things for granted.

But he had considered Michael's feelings; it seemed a good omen. Fortified by that hopeful thought, Abby leaned back in the seat, remembering how startled she'd been when she'd discovered that he and Gemma were distant cousins of the ruler of Dacia.

Gemma had said, 'One of these days I'll take you to see the crown jewels there. They're a magnificent collection of the world's most perfect emeralds.' She'd peered into Abby's face and then sat back, pronouncing, 'In fact, some are exactly the same colour as your eyes. And you'd like the Bagaton cousins. The men are totally, over-the-top gorgeous, and there's a Kiwi connection too. Several—including Prince Luka, the reigning monarch— have married New Zealanders.'

Don't go there! Abby commanded, relieved when Caelan interrupted her memories.

'If you agree, your car can be sold today.'

Her lips tightened. Resentment at being taken over, forced into a situation she couldn't escape, scraped across her nerves. 'I suppose so,' she said colourlessly.

'Yes or no?'

'Yes,' she said between her teeth, and leaned away to point out another, smaller plane beneath them to Michael.

Who crowed with delight before turning a radiant face to the prince to shout, 'Uncle Caelan, look!'

Caelan got to his feet and bent over them to look through the window; Abby caught a faint, masculine scent, and a merciless sexual awareness dazzled her. Her body tightened and her head swam.

Fortunately he straightened up almost immediately, looking down at her with burnished silver-blue eyes, unreadable and hard. 'Breakfast should be ready. I'll go and see.'

Her breath hissed out as he walked to the back of the

plane, his lithe gait a challenge in itself. No wonder he turned up frequently in the gossip columns; he packed a powerful physical charge that overrode all the cautious warnings of her mind.

But at least Gemma had told her what he was—utterly intolerant, quick to judge and incapable of trust. And she'd found out for herself that he was able to effortlessly control his sexual appetite.

It took all of her powers of persuasion to coax Michael back into his seat and buckle him in; his vigorous objections were only halted by the appearance of a middle-aged stewardess carrying a tray. Entranced by this, and the promise of fruit to follow, he settled down to demolish a boiled egg with his usual gusto.

Too strung-up to eat, Abby refused anything apart from a cup of coffee. But it arrived accompanied by thin, crisp toast and several little pots containing a variety of spreads.

'Mr Bagaton said you should have something,' the stewardess explained with a smile.

Abby quelled a frisson of foolish pleasure. His thoughtfulness warmed some small part of her she'd thought permanently frozen.

She looked up as he came back down the aisle, an inchoate smile freezing on her lips when she met a long, watchful inspection that made her acutely aware of the signs of her sleepless night in her face—shadowed eyes, pale skin, and hair like string. Even after combing, it looked the way she'd wanted it to—dull, mousy, boring.

And she didn't—couldn't—allow herself to care what Caelan Bagaton thought of her. Her lips straightened and defiance glittered beneath her lashes as she lifted the coffee-cup to her lips.

No matter what it took, she had to kill this painful

awareness, so intense it had only taken one glance at him to roar into life. In spite of its power and primal force it was meaningless.

Yet, oh, so dangerous.

Caelan transferred his attention to Michael, his mouth curving. 'Are you enjoying your breakfast?'

Trying to ignore the painful twist to her heart, Abby thought cynically that that smile had to be one of the world's great weapons. Michael was no more able to resist it than she was.

A wide grin split Michael's face. 'I had a negg.'

'Was it good?' Caelan lowered his big frame to his seat.

'Yes. And some peaches,' Michael informed him gleefully, and went back to emptying his plate.

But once the tray had been cleared, he began to find the confinement of the seat belt irritating. Abby changed places with him so he could again see out of the window. Obediently he gazed at the lush green countryside that had replaced the stark central plateau beneath, but his interest didn't last long.

Caelan got to his feet, opened the overhead locker and took down the bag she'd packed for just such a moment, but Michael resisted all his favourites with every appearance of loathing.

Not now, she thought wearily. It was too much to expect him to accept the huge change of circumstances without any response, but it would be so much easier if he'd kept the inevitable reaction for later.

Preferably after she'd had a good night's sleep, and with the prince well out of the way!

CHAPTER FOUR

ABBY glanced across the aisle, straight into Caelan's cool, guarded eyes. Hiding her trepidation, she met them with all the composure she could summon, and asked, 'How much longer?'

'About half an hour. Why?'

She inclined her head slightly sideways. 'Energy needs to be expended.'

'He'll have to wait.' Even as she bristled he reached into his narrow leather briefcase and drew out a book she recognised. 'Does he know this?'

'Yes,' she said, truly grateful. 'But we've always had to get it from the library so he'll be more than happy to hear it now.'

How did Caelan know that Michael adored the iconic adventures of a small New Zealand dog? Surely, she thought, going cold, he couldn't have had them investigated that intensively?

Of course he had; a man who thought nothing of infiltrating a child-care centre with an operative to get DNA samples would have insisted on a complete dossier. How else would the stewardess have known that Michael loved peaches?

The thought of such close surveillance sent chills down her spine. Hastily, she opened the book and began to read to an enthralled Michael.

Although the witty, clever exploits of Hairy Maclary and his canine friends did the trick, Abby gave a silent sigh of relief when they finally touched down at the airport in Auckland.

As they made their way to the car park the crowds and the noise and the unfamiliar bustle silenced Michael; wide-eyed, he trailed along between her and the prince, clinging to her hand while he gazed around.

Abby saw a middle-aged woman watching them. Heat stung her skin; she knew what the woman was thinking, just as she recognised the barely concealed interest in other women's eyes when they'd noticed the man beside her. His powerful physical presence demanded instant respect.

Then their eyes swung to her, and envy was replaced by astonishment. They were wondering what on earth a woman like her was doing with a man like Caelan Bagaton.

She wanted to say out loud, 'We're not a family! This is just a sham.' A tormenting sham, one she'd been forced into by the man who'd ruthlessly shattered her life.

Instead, she gave the woman a half-smile and walked on by, her heart contracting into a solid ball in her chest.

'The car's over here,' the prince said brusquely.

The big vehicle had a child's car seat already installed in the rear seat. Naturally, she thought, bristling. Caelan didn't accept defeat.

Stop going over and over and over this, she commanded herself. It's finished—dead as a doornail, or a dodo, or the Dead Sea. All of them, actually.

At first Michael was too interested in the traffic—especially, Abby noted with wry amusement, extremely large trucks—to get bored. However, by the time the car left the motorway for inner-city streets he demanded in a voice that came too close to a whine, 'Where we going, Abby? Are we nearly there?'

'Five minutes,' Caelan said calmly.

So he wasn't taking them to the beach house, where he'd kissed her.

She fought a humiliating let-down; he probably didn't even remember that kiss. After all, he'd had at least one long-term relationship since he'd broken up with the then-current lover. And Gemma had told her of the constant stream of hopefuls he fended off. The kiss they'd shared probably no longer registered on his radar—if it ever had.

Pinning a steady smile to her lips, she said to Michael, 'There you go—we're almost at Uncle Caelan's house.'

'It's an apartment,' Caelan informed her.

'An apartment?' Abby shot a swift glance at his unyielding profile. In a neutral voice she said, 'Children need easy access to grass and trees, and a place where they can run and jump and roll.'

'All highly desirable, but not as necessary as decent food and clothes and security,' Caelan returned, his urbane tone not hiding the whiplash of scorn in his words. 'The apartment is central and convenient, but if it doesn't work out we'll move to somewhere more suitable for a family.' Skilfully he eased the car past a courier van.

She frowned to hide a suddenly thudding heartbeat. A family...

In spite of her effort to be reasonable, anticipation warmed her from the inside, curling through her like warm honey shot with fire. To quell it she asked more aggressively than she intended, 'But you told Michael on the flight that you have a pool.' And then she remembered an article she'd seen about a very up-market apartment complex in Auckland. 'Oh, is there a gym there?'

'There's a lap pool on the terrace.'

She flushed. His casual words underlined again the

huge difference between growing up on a Northland citrus orchard, and amongst the ranks of the hugely rich.

Expertly Caelan avoided three laughing teenagers who chose to dash across the road as the lights turned green. 'And of course there's the one at the beach.'

So he did still own it.

A wild, foolish second of elation was rapidly smothered by another cold splash of common sense. How pathetic was that—thinking that one kiss might have meant anything to him? Turning to Michael, she infused enthusiasm into her voice. 'Just about there, darling.'

Very much there, in fact; the car stopped outside a gate that led to a basement car park. Absently Abby read a notice on the wall, then stiffened.

'This is a hotel,' she accused.

The gate rattled back and Caelan put the car into gear, easing it down into the well-lit basement. 'An apartment hotel. I live in the penthouse.'

Michael asked with eager anticipation, 'Can I go for a swim, Abby? Now?'

He adored the water; the day-care centre had a small paddling pool, but Abby had never been able to afford lessons for him in the school pool.

'Sweetheart, I think it would be better if you left it until it's warmer,' she told him. Although nowhere near as cold as Nukuroa, Auckland's spring wasn't exactly balmy, and at the airport she'd noticed a brisk, cool wind.

His lower lip jutted, but Caelan cut short his objections. 'The pool is heated, and sheltered from the wind. I'll go in with him if you don't want to.'

Well, yes, she thought cynically, of course it would be heated. Standard tycoon equipment!

The car came to a halt in a reserved slot. Abby tamped down a flare of anger; she'd been making decisions for

Michael for three years, and Caelan had no right to query them.

In a toneless voice she answered, 'If it's heated, that's fine. Unfortunately he's absolutely fearless in the water, although he hasn't got beyond the fundamentals yet. He needs careful supervision.'

'Point taken. He'd better learn to swim as soon as possible.' Caelan switched off the engine.

Abby examined the autocratic lines and curves of his profile as he said, 'The pool is fenced off from the apartment, so he'll be safe enough.'

Physically, yes. Emotionally? Ignoring a cold little worm of fear, she told herself sturdily that all she could hope to extract from this tensely disturbing situation was Michael's happiness.

Inside the hotel lift, a warm little hand clutching hers, Abby stared blindly at the carpet, alienated by the atmosphere of sleek, elegant luxury. A faint scent permeated the air—a very exclusive, very expensive perfume; disliking its cloying sensuousness, Abby wrinkled her nose and tried to ignore an alarming needle of jealousy.

The atmosphere was compounded inside the penthouse apartment. Of course it was elegant and large, filled with reflected light from the harbour and the sky, and superbly decorated by a professional who hadn't surrendered comfort for style.

The prince took them into a large, informal sitting room with a dining table and chairs at one end. It opened out onto a wide, partly covered terrace where potted plants flourished around a narrow swimming pool.

'There's another, more formal sitting room through that door, but I use it mainly for entertaining,' he told her. 'This one is more suitable for a child.'

'It's lovely,' she murmured, walking across to a row

of windows at the end. Startled, she looked straight into the harbour, as though they were on the bow of an ocean liner.

From behind Caelan said, 'The hotel is built on one of the wharves.'

A fat ferry bumbled purposefully towards the North Shore; it reminded Abby of a beetle and she smiled involuntarily.

'The kitchen is through that door,' he said crisply. 'Do you want a drink? No? Then I'll show you your rooms.'

Michael's was the first. Abby had expected an exercise in sleek minimalism, but this was a young boy's dream, a circus fantasy with a tasselled tent top and a frieze of prancing animals.

Oh, Caelan had been utterly and completely confident that he'd be bringing Michael back with him! And why not? He held all the cards.

'Your room is next door, you share a bathroom,' he told Abby, indicating a door. He glanced at his watch and frowned. 'I have to check out a few things, so I'll leave you to explore by yourselves for ten minutes or so. Your luggage has arrived, so you'll be able to change into your togs, Michael.'

Left alone with a silent, fascinated Michael, Abby admired a magnificently prancing rocking-horse. At the back of her mind she wondered how many women had come to this penthouse and been swept off their feet by their host's potent sexuality.

Droves, she thought savagely. A small voice insisting on being taken to the bathroom put a welcome end to her thoughts. She gave Michael a swift hug and showed him where it was.

Then they explored the room next door, furnished in restful, sophisticated shades of sand with a throw rug of deep rust lending richness to the neutral scheme. A chair and a desk against one wall were set out for writing; a daybed in the window suggested long afternoons of reading. Abby's gaze lingered on a vase of orchids, exquisite fly-away things in shades of caramel, rust and golden-green.

Had Caelan chosen them? Highly unlikely, she decided. No doubt a florist kept each of the rooms in this luxurious place filled with blooms that matched the décor as perfectly as those orchids did.

Well, she'd far rather have a handful of dandelions picked from the paddock and given to her in a chubby little hand.

'Where does Uncle Caelan sleep?' Michael asked, looking around.

'I don't know,' Abby said crisply. Not at this end of the penthouse, anyway. Possibly he had a suite well away from his guest rooms. 'Come on, we'd better find your swimming togs.'

Ten minutes later, Caelan knocked on the door. Made exuberant by excitement, Michael rushed across to open it.

Abby's stomach lurched and that treacherous flow of anticipation turned into sharp, painful awareness. In swimming shorts, a large towel draped over one copper-bronze, sleekly muscled shoulder, Caelan's compelling physicality cut through centuries of civilised conditioning. In spite of every barrier she'd constructed, the primitive instinct to mate with the most alpha male flamed into life within her.

'Do you have a towel?' he asked, smiling as his nephew jumped around him like a puppy.

Michael grabbed it up from the bed and went off without a backwards glance, chattering and animated. Feeling resentfully like an unwanted extra, Abby followed them out onto a wide terrace overlooking the harbour and the North Shore.

She sat down in a lounger beneath a sail that kept the hot northern sun from her head, and watched intently as the two men now in her life stopped by the gate into the pool enclosure. The light in this sub-tropical part of New Zealand was softer, more humid than in the south, smoothing over Caelan's torso to delineate every coiled muscle as he stooped to speak to his nephew. Broad-shouldered, narrow-hipped and with the innate grace of a leopard, he looked dangerous and dynamic and fascinating.

Furious at the slow burn of desire in the pit of her stomach, she thought acidly that Mediterranean heritage had a lot to answer for. No doubt the splash of Celtic blood that had given him his name and his ice-blue eyes had provided the long, powerful legs, but his formidable confidence and authority were his own.

She must never allow herself to forget that Caelan used his tough tenacity and ruthless intelligence—and his charisma—like weapons. He was a warrior, gathering the fruits of war.

In which quest it probably helped that he didn't have a heart. In fact, it surprised her that he had enough glimmerings of conscience to feel responsible for Gemma's son.

No, that was unfair; even Gemma had admitted that her half-brother was meticulous in fulfilling his obligations. In fact, it had been one of the reasons she'd demanded Abby's promise.

'I don't want Michael to be a duty like I was,' she'd said flatly. 'He'd be just another project to see through to completion. Oh, Caelan would do his best for him, but it's not enough to know you're no more than a responsibility.'

The early death of his father had pitched Caelan into the cut-throat arena of international business in his mid-twenties, and, to most people's astonishment, he'd succeeded wildly. At the same time he'd taken charge of his impulsive, wilful sister.

His best hadn't been good enough for Gemma; she'd make sure he dealt better with Michael, Abby decided, her gaze following them into the pool enclosure. Excitement raised Michael's voice higher than usual against his uncle's deeper tones. The elusive resemblance between them tugged at her heartstrings.

Oh, Gemma, she thought forlornly, I'll look after him whatever happens, but I feel very outgunned right now!

And then she stiffened her spine in a determination that masked a deep, abiding dread. There was much more than her happiness at stake; weigh her wary, reluctant attraction against a child's future, and that feverish tug at her senses meant very little.

And as she clearly wasn't necessary here, she should really go and unpack Michael's clothes.

Instead, she leaned back into the sleek, luxuriously comfortable lounger to watch. Against the shimmer of the water in the bright spring sun, Caelan crouched by his nephew and began to talk. Abby watched Michael's face, solemn and intent as he nodded.

Straining her ears, she heard Caelan say, 'And no jumping in.'

'No jumping,' Michael repeated, a little disappointed but resigned.

'Only if I'm there to catch you. Wait until I'm in the water, and I'll tell you when to jump.'

After another serious nod Michael gave a great beaming smile, twisting Abby's heart. Both were feeling their way; Michael was prepared to like the man who'd appeared out of the darkness, and so far Caelan had settled for treating his nephew like a small adult.

An attitude that made Michael blossom, she noted with another despicable stab of jealousy.

Glass panels sheltered both pool and terrace from the cool breeze that trailed in off the harbour. When the two swimmers got into the water her heart—foolish organ!—contracted even more tightly as Michael imitated everything the prince did. She kept a close eye on them, only relaxing when she saw that Caelan was always near enough to rescue his nephew from any risky exploits.

Their laughter blended, and a great weariness weighed down her eyelids. She'd cope, but first she had to accept that her life had changed irrevocably. From now on it wouldn't be just her and Michael against the world; Caelan had altered the balance, and nothing would ever be the same.

Michael had someone else to rely on, and she'd just have to accept it.

Too soon, so swiftly she wasn't aware of what was happening, Abby's wakeful night caught up with her and she slid into darkness.

Michael's voice woke her, soft and urgent in her ear. 'Abby, Abby, wake up now.'

After a prodigious yawn, she said, 'What's the time, darling—?'

And remembered where she was.

Her eyelids jerked up, but she was no longer lying in the lounger by the pool; instead, she was curled up on the bed in the room Caelan had given her, the rust-red wrap covering her.

Fully dressed in T-shirt and shorts, his hair dry, Michael stood beside it, and behind him loomed Caelan—who must have carried her in and put her there. She could see the knowledge in his expression, a subtle tension and awareness that stoked her own mindless response to him.

Head whirling, she got up on her elbow and swung her legs onto the floor. 'What time is it?' she asked thinly.

She sounded slack, almost drugged. Caelan scrutinised her face, but the colour flooded back into her skin as she straightened. He tried to ignore the sensuous memory of her sleek body in his arms, her breathing when she'd snuggled her cheek against his chest. Yet other images prowled his brain, images snatched from barely remembered dreams in which she'd lain beneath him, soft and warm and silken, of little gasping cries as she climaxed around him, the scent of her skin and the perfumed cloud of her hair, the way her voice changed from crisp confidence to an enchanting husky shyness when he'd made love to her, the way she laughed—

How the hell could one kiss four years ago light the need and hunger that still burned like a fire underground?

He'd never stopped wanting her, he admitted, and never stopped resenting the power she wielded over him.

So he should do something about sating this damned inconvenient desire.

She was watching him, her face guarded and stubborn, but in spite of her prickly demeanour he was too experienced not to recognise the unwanted tug of attraction. Everything pointed to it—her careful avoidance of his touch, the soft flutter of her pulse at the base of her throat whenever he came near her, and the colour that came and went in her silky, seductive skin.

A plan that had occurred to him as they'd flown up solidified in his mind.

In spite of his best attempt at control, his voice was rough when he told her, 'Almost one o'clock. I wouldn't have woken you, but I have an appointment shortly.'

'One o'clock?' She pushed back a tumbling lock of hair and asked swiftly, 'Has Michael had his lunch?'

'Yes. Peanut butter sandwiches,' Caelan returned with a faint smile.

She hid another yawn behind her hand. 'His staple food,' she said in a wry voice.

'He also had half an orange and a glass of milk.'

Abby nodded. 'Give me five minutes. I need to wash my face.'

It took a little longer than that, because she had a rapid shower in the sybaritic bathroom, all glass and tiled walls with equipment that looked as though it fitted out a spaceship. Spirits marginally boosted by a change of clothes, she closed the bedroom door behind her and followed the sound of voices to the living room off the kitchen.

She'd almost got there when Caelan laughed, for once without the undernote of cynicism she'd always heard.

But when she came into the room all humour vanished from his strong face. He said aloofly, 'I'll be back around six this evening. Don't worry about dinner; we can order from the hotel menu.'

'What about Michael?' she said steadily. 'I don't imagine the hotel kitchen caters to children his age.'

'It can, but check out the fridge.' He ruffled Michael's hair, smiled down into his face and looked up to assess Abby with hard blue eyes. Very casually, he finished, 'Don't try leaving the apartment.'

'Why?'

'You both need time to get your bearings.' He paused before saying deliberately, 'It would be inconvenient if I had to go out looking for you.'

The warning was no less intimidating for being implied rather than stated forcefully. Her stomach a tight, apprehensive knot, she watched him leave, grateful when a question from Michael broke into her thoughts.

'Abby, can we swim again now?'

'After you've had your nap,' she said automatically, and concealed her furious resentment by opening the refrigerator.

Of course it was filled with eminently suitable food for a hungry three-year-old. After a molten survey of the interior, Abby almost slammed the enormous door shut. Whatever else he was—or wasn't—Caelan was a superb organiser. No doubt if she tried to leave the apartment someone would stop her, or accompany her.

She didn't need the humiliation.

Still fuming, she spent the hour of Michael's nap unpacking, grimacing at the pathetic show her few dreary clothes made in a wardrobe almost as big as Michael's bedroom in the cottage. They were so out of context they looked ludicrous.

Growing up she'd known comfort and security, but the luxury Caelan took for granted was completely alien to her.

'That's what you get for getting in the way of a dominant alpha male,' she told herself. Money and power had helped forge his intimidating inner confidence, but mix with a brilliant mind and loads of disturbing male magnetism, spice the whole mix with a soupçon of princely blood, season with a hint of Latin—and you had Caelan Bagaton, one on his own.

Once Michael woke, they explored his room, discovering a box of toys to go with the rocking-horse, and a whole new library of books. Abby thought of the tattered, much-read volumes she'd packed, and wondered whether Michael would want to read them again.

They spent the rest of the lazy afternoon out on the terrace with books, blocks and crayons until, when the sun began its slow slide down towards the west, she braved the unknown terrors of the impressive stove in the kitchen.

She was bathing Michael when Caelan arrived. To her astonishment he came into the bathroom as though he were accustomed to such familiar rituals, not even grimacing when Michael slipped as he was getting out and sent a tidal wave of water onto his uncle's superbly cut shirt and trousers.

'Careful,' Abby said, more sharply than she'd intended.

Horrified, Michael flushed and screwed up his face. 'I'm sorry, I didn't mean to.'

Caelan said mildly, 'I know that.' And was rewarded with a shy smile.

A pang of dislocation and guilt hit Abby. She dried Michael down, stuffed him into his pyjamas and tried hard not to feel left out when Michael asked that Caelan read his bedtime story. At least he'd chosen one of his old favourites, not the glossy new ones Caelan had provided. As she heard Caelan provide a spirited rendition of an old fairy tale she decided that he must have been practising...

Then he bent his head for Michael's goodnight kiss as though he'd been doing it all his life.

At last, leaving Michael safely tucked up in bed and supervised by a brand new state-of-the-art monitor, Caelan escorted her into the living room.

'I'll get you a drink,' he said. 'Is it still white wine?'

She nodded, although it had been four years since she'd tasted any.

As he poured he said levelly, 'You look triste. What is it?'

She shut down her emotions, hoping her face was a composed mask. 'Just thinking.'

Apart from the child sleeping in his bed, they were alone in the apartment. That dangerous, mindless excitement was stirring in her body, basic and inescapable as the breath in her lungs and the blood that raced through her veins.

Handing her the glass, Caelan said, 'I've already ordered dinner; it arrives in half an hour. Until then, try to relax.'

Relax? He had to be mad! She looked up, but his expression was coolly noncommittal, his eyes transparent and slightly amused.

Baffled and angry, she evaded the hidden tension by walking through the long glass doors onto the terrace.

The swift northern dusk had turned into night; beyond the safety-glass balustrade the harbour gleamed like black satin, and the North Shore suburbs sparkled against the bulk of Rangitoto, Auckland's iconic island volcano. A small breeze carried the scent of the sea to her, ghosting over her sensitised skin. Feeling utterly forlorn, she shivered.

She didn't belong to Caelan's world of privilege and sophistication and wealth, of ancient aristocratic bloodlines and power. Responding to him in any way was not only stupid, it was humiliating and pathetic and embarrassing.

Her lips widened in a bleak, mirthless smile and she

swung around to look at the Harbour Bridge, a shallow arc of lights reflected in the water.

She sipped some of the exquisitely fragrant wine. Just when she sensed that Caelan had followed her out she had no idea; the knowledge of his presence came as a feather of response down her spine, a slow conviction that escalated the turmoil inside her.

Heart jumping, tense as a stretched wire, she hurried into speech, choosing the most innocuous subject that came to mind. 'What made you decide to live here?'

'I travel a lot, so the chopper pad at Mechanic's Bay is handy for quick trips to the airport.'

Moving slowly, she turned her head a few degrees to see him. Unwanted, unbidden, a memory surfaced. Once—in another lifetime—she'd ruffled his black hair, fascinated by its silken warmth. Her fingers tingled as though they'd been deprived, and her heart jolted in her breast. Breath came fast through her lips, and she shuddered at the seductive impact of the forgotten sensation.

And then she met his eyes, and every languorous memory disappeared; nothing could survive in the frigid wasteland of his gaze.

Angry with herself for her chagrin, she said, 'Michael loved the toys and the books. Thank you.' Even though she suspected that Caelan had consulted an expert, it had to be said.

'And the horse?'

She said, 'He's most impressed, and is taking his time to get to know it.'

His broad shoulders lifted negligently. 'It's the one I had as a child. I had a craftsman in Northland repair and refurbish it. I'm glad another child will ride it.'

He was pointing out the difference between what she had given Michael, and what he could give. Meeting the subtle implication head-on, she said clearly, 'Too many toys aren't good for children. Michael hasn't missed anything in his life except parents.'

He said coolly, 'And his uncle. Why did you decide to leave Nukuroa?'

The eerie wail of a siren somewhere close by cut into the tense pause that followed Caelan's words. Abby covered an uneasy movement with another sip of her drink.

In the end she admitted, 'I felt—stalked. And I've learned to trust my instincts. How did you find us?'

'I've had an investigator looking for you ever since you arrived in New Zealand with Michael,' he said, adding abruptly, 'He seems a happy, secure child, and for that I thank you.'

Made more uncomfortable by his rare softening than by his open contempt, she muttered, 'You don't need to thank me.' And because she wanted to get things settled, she went on abruptly, 'You said yesterday—was it yesterday?—that we'd work out some sort of arrangement for this situation when I was less emotional. Exactly what do you have in mind for this—for our lives?'

He set his glass down on a nearby table and examined her face, remote in the darkness, with eyes she couldn't see. 'Have you decided to stop resisting the inevitable?'

'I—yes, I have.' Although she was quaking inside, pride steadied her voice and gave an edge to her words. 'As you pointed out so cogently, I don't have any choice. You have power and money and I have none. And you could send me to prison if you press charges against me for claiming Michael as my son.'

He accepted that as the simple statement of fact it was. 'You have power too. You're the only mother Michael's ever known. For his sake, I suggest we try to make this as normal a relationship as possible.'

What did he mean by that? A kind of panicky antici-pation set her nerves sizzling. Avoiding his eyes, she said, 'Explain normal.'

And relationship!

His mouth twisted mockingly. 'It's quite simple. We marry.'

CHAPTER FIVE

ABBY'S jaw dropped. 'We—*what*?' she said faintly, her brain empty of anything but shock. Blinking fiercely to stop Caelan's dark, sardonic face wavering in front of her dazed eyes, she croaked, 'What did you say?'

'You heard.' The cynical amusement in his tone rubbed her nerves raw. 'It's the most sensible thing to do.'

Stunned, Abby stared at him, her emotions spinning in endless free fall. 'The most sensible thing to do?' she parroted, sounding both feeble and incredulous, heart thudding sickly as though she stood on the brink of a precipice.

'For Michael,' Caelan agreed courteously, although the amusement in his voice rubbed her pride raw. 'For everyone, in fact.'

Her teeth snapped shut on an unwise retort. Disgusted with the treacherous heat that surged through her, she dragged in a jagged breath. 'I'd sacrifice a lot for Michael,' she said, her voice a brittle thread in the silence, 'but I won't marry you for him. The idea is outrageous.'

'Only if you view it emotionally.' His deep voice was so completely empty of feeling that she shivered.

'*Any* way you view it.'

He shrugged, every angle and plane of his hard face radiating tough self-assurance. 'Michael is a Bagaton. I want his status regularised. Gemma was proud of her heritage—she'd want it too.'

71

Abby bit her lip. Oh, he knew where to aim his arrows!

Before she could formulate the objections buzzing around her brain Caelan said, 'I've taken legal opinion on this. The simplest way to achieve his correct surname is for us to marry.'

Suspiciously she asked, 'That's all?'

'Not quite. We then apply to adopt him.'

'Surely you do the applying,' she returned swiftly, her suspicion growing. 'He's already registered as my son.'

'That doesn't count. As the law in New Zealand stands, both of us need to adopt him.' When she was silent he said indifferently, 'I'll find a decent lawyer for you to consult if you don't believe me.'

Almost she said that it didn't matter, but perhaps that was the reaction he was hoping for. 'That's an excellent idea,' she said tonelessly.

'We'll need to convince the welfare authorities that we'll be good parents, but I doubt there'll be any difficulty about that. Naturally the main criterion will be a solid, loving home life for him.' He paused, before adding deliberately, 'Once the adoptions are formalised, you won't have to face the prospect of losing him, and I won't worry about him ending up in the clutches of the social welfare system.'

Abby flashed a swift, startled glance at him. 'Why would he do that?'

'There's the small matter of you claiming him as your child. As you acknowledged, forging documents can earn you a prison offence.'

She went white. 'Are you threatening me?'

'No.' He went on in a pragmatic tone that iced her blood. 'But any writer ferreting around in Palaweyo is almost certain to discover that Michael is Gemma's child, so your actions could come to the notice of the authorities in New Zealand. The sooner we get married and set the wheels in motion for adoption, the better, because an adoption can't be negated.'

Trying to think clearly, Abby said numbly, 'I—yes, I see.' Shattered, she dragged breath into her compressed lungs. 'You're sure of all this?'

His eyes met hers, cold, completely level, utterly convincing. 'Yes.'

Oddly enough she believed him. She pushed a shaky hand through her hair and wondered how he could sound so casual when he was suggesting such a complete disruption to his life. And hers.

The thought of being married to him made her quake inside. She'd tried so hard to do what Gemma had asked, and it seemed it was all for nothing—but at least this way she'd be there to look after Michael.

If she didn't end up in prison.

Even if that happened, she thought painfully, there were worse things than being looked after by a nanny—being lost in the welfare system, for one, as Caelan had pointed out.

The silence grew, backgrounded by the slow hum of traffic and music drifting up from somewhere in the hotel. Slow, moody, erotically charged, it brushed across her skin, tightening it and alerting her senses to the overpoweringly male presence of the man watching her.

In the end she said wearily, 'If it safeguards Michael then I'll—I'll marry you.'

The prince didn't gloat. Instead he said, 'I'll ring my cousin tonight.'

She stared blankly at him. 'What?'

One black brow rose. 'My cousin Luka rules Dacia. We'll be married there.'

'In Dacia?' she said foolishly, panic surging up to kick

her in the stomach. 'Surely a quiet private wedding here…' Her voice trailed away.

'We'll do that before we leave for Dacia so that we can set the adoption in motion immediately.'

She pushed a shaking hand across her forehead. 'Two marriages?' she said thinly. 'It seems overkill.'

'For Michael's sake we need to make a statement to the world.' His face hardened when her lips formed a silent negative. Ruthlessly overriding her objections he stated, 'It's a family tradition to marry in Dacia, and, looked at from a purely practical point of view, my cousin can control the media there. My family will want to meet you, and there will be a series of celebrations. The Dacians are a warm-hearted people, and they enjoy weddings.'

Desperately she broke in. 'I can cope with this—with anything—in New Zealand, but I'm not the sort of person you should marry, and you know it. I'd be out of my element with your relatives, and they'd have every right to wonder what on earth you're doing bringing me into the family.'

'They wouldn't dare,' he said forcefully. 'Anyway, that's not their style. You're not out of your element with me, are you?'

Oh, if only he knew! She flung the truth at him. 'Of course I am!'

His eyes gleamed with amusement. 'Rubbish. And you dealt with Gemma. If you can cope with us, you can cope with anyone else you might meet.'

Abby picked up her glass and took a large sip of wine. 'This is just a nightmare, right?' she said hopefully when she could speak again. 'We're really going to get married quietly at the beach house with two witnesses, and I'll never have to meet any of your family.'

He gave a swift mirthless smile. 'The beach house part, yes—three days from now, in fact. The family—you don't know the Bagatons if you think they'll be content to ignore my marriage.'

Turmoil churned inside her, a mixture of scared apprehension salted with a hot excitement she despised. She swivelled away and stared out across the harbour. High above them a thin moon curled against the depthless sky; Rangitoto loomed to the east, still and dark and silent, as though it had never filled the sky with fire. If she turned her head she could see a number of other small dark hills, their conical shapes all proclaiming their violent origins.

She said on a long, harsh sigh, 'That's the point, surely? I *don't* know the Bagatons—in fact, apart from you and Gemma, I've never met anyone with a drop of royal blood.'

'You're almost certainly wrong there,' he said, more cool amusement grating across her nerves like emery paper. 'It's far more common than you think. You probably have more than a drop yourself.'

'If so, it's from the wrong side of the blanket.' She muttered hopelessly, 'I don't believe this.'

His voice hardened. 'Believe it. And just to make sure that no rumours reach the welfare agencies here, we need to convince everyone we meet that this is a love match.'

By now too numb to react, she asked, 'Why?'

He shrugged, broad shoulders cutting out the lights of Harbour Bridge. 'We're sacrificing our freedom to provide Michael with the stability and love he needs. I don't see us being able to reassure a social worker that we've got a good marriage while you and I are circling each other like wolves on the prowl.'

Heart jolting, Abby took a step backwards, but Caelan's lean fingers snaked around her wrist, pulling her towards him with a smile that blended desire and calculation.

Abby's senses rioted, savouring his unique aroma, an erotic mixture of heat and masculinity. She searched his face, eyes widening at the glitter of desire firing ice-blue eyes, the predatory curve of his bold mouth. Oh, God, he was going to kiss her, and if he did—what hope did she have of standing against him?

A wild mixture of searing anticipation and terror almost silenced her, but she managed to protest, 'No!'

'Then we might as well call a halt to this right now.'

His aloof, studied tone set her stomach roiling, almost banishing the excitement of his nearness. He had to feel the betraying turmoil in her pulse, because one lean, tanned finger was stroking across the fine blue veins in her wrist. Her will-power wavered and dissolved under a wave of desire so intense she could feel it scorching away every sensible thought.

But she had to corral the thoughts blundering around her brain. He had money and influence, and she had none. He was offering a settled life for Michael, his rightful place in the world and security.

And parents, a family…

Nevertheless, she pushed a lock of hair back from her forehead and said hoarsely, 'Caelan, it won't work.'

He looked at her with a cool irony that hurt far more than his contempt. 'Frustration makes people unreasonable and stupid. You want me, as I want you. Whatever else has changed, that hasn't. Four years ago the kiss we exchanged told me we'd be good together.' His voice deepened, a raw note appearing beneath the words. 'And you knew it too. It's still there, so why should we deny ourselves?'

And then he pulled her into his arms and his mouth

came down on hers in a kiss that was more than erotic; it registered a primal claim, fundamental and exhilarating and utterly compelling.

Abby melted, wild hunger shutting down everything but the delight of Caelan's mouth on hers, effortlessly working a dark enchantment that fogged her brain and loosened the reins of her will-power.

When her mouth opened to his demand he took instant possession of its depths, exploring with a carnal, leisurely expertise that sent a current of delicious hunger through every cell. He tasted so good, she thought exultantly, a slow, dangerous pulse flowering deep in her pelvis. After the long, empty years she was where she belonged, with Caelan.

Without volition, her free hand lifted, coming to rest over his heart; it beat heavily, unsteadily, driving into her palm with a clamorous force. Sensation stormed through her, sweet as honey, potent as wine, fierce as a bushfire.

But apart from his lips and the loop of fingers around her wrist he wasn't touching her. Desperately she jerked her head free and stared up into his eyes, and the heat in her body congealed into chilly emptiness. Silence stretched between them, jagged with unspoken thoughts and emotions.

'No,' she grated, scarcely aware of what she was refusing.

He'd set out to prove that he wielded a sorcerer's power over her, and she'd just delivered the proof, signed, sealed and gift-wrapped. Despising herself, she twisted away, humiliated afresh when he let her go as though it had meant nothing to him.

His next words astonished her. 'Still the same flash-fire of passion,' he said in a voice that couldn't hide the intensity of the words. 'Sex has a lot to answer for. Did I hurt your wrist?'

'What?' She looked down, flushing when she realised she was massaging the fragile skin there. Dropping both hands to her sides, she said through lips that were tender and full, branded by his kiss, 'No, it's all right.' Pride drove her to articulate the next words with cold clarity in spite of the bitter turmoil inside her. 'I'm not in the market for an exorcism, Caelan.'

The heat in his eyes was swallowed by darkness. 'Is that what it would be?' he said. 'Somehow I don't believe it's going to be that easy. Or even necessary.'

With the flimsy safety of a few feet between them, Abby closed her eyes and took a deep breath, calling on anger to replace the sensual chains of desire.

'I refuse to be your legal mistress.' Everything that made marriage special—love, trust, determination to make it work, emotional commitment—would be absent, and all they'd have in common was that flash-fire of passion, as he'd called it. But really it was lust.

'That's a different way of looking at marriage.' His voice deepened into a sexy rumble. 'I can promise you that any pleasure will be mutual.'

Oh, God, she was so tempted to give into desire, to forget everything but this need pulsing through her, a wanton hunger that sliced through the fabric of her fragile composure, highlighting promised sexual delights with the emphasis of memory...

You're forgetting Michael, her mind prompted her.

She had to clamp her mouth shut to keep the words of surrender unsaid. When her lashes lifted she saw Caelan smile—all hard derision, but the blue heat she remembered so well still gleamed in the depths of his eyes.

'Mutual pleasure?' She managed to produce some sort of scorn in her tone.

'However much you despise yourself for wanting that pleasure, it means that with our common concern for Michael we can build some sort of life together.'

Bitterly, she answered, 'There's a lot more to marriage than sex. What about trust?'

His lashes hooded his eyes. 'Trust is an entirely different thing,' he said indifferently. 'It has to be earned.'

Temper, hot and reviving, flared into action, temporarily masking the dangerous flare of passion. 'So I'm on probation? For the rest of my life, I suppose.'

He shrugged negligently. 'Once Michael's grown up you can do what you like.' But there was nothing negligent about his next words. They echoed with cold menace. 'Keep in mind that I don't share. If you stray, I'll make your life so unpleasant that you'll beg to be free of me—even if it means leaving Michael.'

White-lipped, she flung back, 'You just don't understand, do you? Nothing would make me abandon him—*nothing*.' Sheer temper spurred her on. 'When I make promises I keep them. And while we're living together, I'll expect you to be faithful too. When you kissed me at the beach you were another woman's lover.'

Colour burned along his magnificent cheekbones. 'I broke it off the next day,' he grated. 'I intend to remain faithful.'

'Why should I believe you?' She whirled around and stalked across to the balustrade, staring down at the lights shimmering across the water for taut seconds before turning to say defiantly, 'I don't want to make love with you. Not now, not at some later date—not ever.'

'You do, but you're not ready to admit it yet,' he said

with an unruffled detachment that made her feel over-emotional and foolish.

At her disbelieving snort he said flatly, 'I feel that way too—like a lesser person because I seem to be unable to control this hunger.' His voice turned flinty. 'I'm no monster, Abby. I can wait until you're ready.'

Until you surrender, he meant.

Aching as though she'd been defeated in a physical fight, she said numbly, 'I don't want any dinner. I'll go to bed.'

Caelan glanced at his watch. 'Run away by all means—but your meal will be here in ten minutes. I'll bring it to your room. And you'd better eat it—starving yourself won't win you any sympathy from me.'

He waited until she got to the door before saying, 'Before you go—'

Abby paused, but fixed her gaze on the door handle.

'Two things—wash that damned dye out of your hair.'

Rebellion churned through her, but she asked distantly, 'And the second order?'

'Don't try to leave,' he advised. 'You won't get far. And if you do, all bargains are off.'

'As you've pointed out, I don't have any choice, do I?' she said starkly, burning with resentment.

He waited long enough to tighten her every nerve with unbearable tension before saying with an indifference that cut her as much as his contempt, 'No. Everyone has to live with the results of the choices they've made.'

Silently she walked out and closed the door behind her.

But once inside her alien, luxurious room her shoulders slumped. Tears aching behind her eyes, she wondered why she felt so desolated.

Why had she flung down that ridiculous gauntlet about

not wanting to make love with him? He must know she had no defences against her overwhelming need for him.

Four years ago, dazzled and unwary, she'd been intrigued by him. Only too aware of his reputation, she'd fought her craving.

At least his kiss had jolted her out of that! Terrified by her capacity for feeling, she'd panicked, but for months on Palaweyo she'd dreamed that he'd followed her. Fortunately—and inevitably—he hadn't. Instead, he'd found a new love—an enormously talented writer notorious for her fascinating, sensual poetry and unrestrained enjoyment of life.

Mouth turned down at the corners, Abby strode into the bathroom. How stupidly innocent she'd been. And how ridiculous she was being now!

OK, so she'd been sure she was over him. Naturally, when she discovered that in less than twenty-four hours that violent, mindless attraction had rekindled, she was concerned.

Stopping in front of the mirror she stared at her reflection with smoky, dazed eyes. Unwittingly she touched her lips, soft and red and still trembling from Caelan's kiss.

Concerned, she taunted silently—what sort of word was that? She wasn't concerned—she was *terrified*. How could he shatter her defences with just one kiss?

If she married him, inevitably she'd give in to that wildfire hunger. What then? Did he want children from her, or would Michael be enough? The thought of bearing Caelan's child produced an odd pang somewhere in the region of her heart. Then there was the social thing—their marriage would stun his rarefied world of aristocrats and magnates, causing a firestorm of gossip.

She'd be the maverick in his select retinue of sophisticated, experienced, beautiful women, all of whom had been sensible enough not to expect love from him. Not that he was a playboy; in spite of her accusation, he'd been faithful to each of his mistresses—a serial monogamist, she thought, trying to soothe her jangling nerves with common sense.

'What am I going to do?' she whispered, seeking counsel from her reflection.

The woman in the mirror stared wildly, helplessly back until a firm tap on the bathroom door stopped the breath in her throat.

'Your meal's waiting,' Caelan said. 'Eat it.'

Battered by emotion, as though his kiss had stripped a protective skin away to leave her defenceless and naked, she swung around and waited until she was sure he'd left the room. Even then, she eased the door open.

Of course he'd gone.

After eating as much as she could of food that tasted like ashes, she had to force herself to take the tray into the kitchen. There was no sign of Caelan, although she could hear him speaking, his deep voice articulating with swift firmness. He was on the telephone, she realised, and thrust the remainders of the food into the fridge so she could flee back to her room before he finished the call.

Once in its sanctuary, she washed her hair, watching colour stream down the plug until the golden-amber of her own colouring shone through. Even wet, her hair still looked dull, its vibrant gloss banished by the dye. She picked up the conditioner in the shower, nodding when she saw the name.

Only the best for Prince Caelan Bagaton, she thought sardonically, and slathered the liquid on, letting hot, slow tears run down her cheeks.

Then she tried to shower the effects of his kiss from

her sensitised body, staying in so long her fingers wrinkled.

Once out and in the oversized T-shirt she wore to bed, she checked Michael, blissfully asleep. She lingered a few moments, watching him before bending to kiss his cheek and heading back into her own room.

Exhausted, she wanted nothing more than to crawl beneath the covers and fall headlong into sleep, but she sat down on the side of the bed and stared sightlessly around the stylish, expensive room while memories replayed in her head and her body ached for a banished ecstasy.

So now Caelan knew—they both knew—that the sexual link between them was as compelling and intense as it had been four years before.

Abby straightened her shoulders. Obsessively going over and over what had happened years ago solved nothing; she had something much more contemporary to deal with.

Caelan had re-ignited a fire deep inside her, a fire she'd thought long dead, but the real danger wasn't the untamed, elemental hunger in his eyes, the raw urgency of his kiss. No, the true peril lay in her fierce response.

She had so pathetically few defences against his passion.

'So,' she said aloud, trying to convince herself, 'it must never happen again.'

The practical part of her mind scoffed.

Whatever price she had to pay, she thought defiantly, was worth it to keep Michael safe. Shivering, she crawled into bed, trying to empty her mind.

Eventually, after hours of listening to the night sounds of the city, devouring sleep replaced her darting, frightened thoughts with dreams.

* * *

Night should have brought some ease of mind. It didn't; when she woke she felt as though her life had been dumped into a blender.

Until an eager little voice from the door asked interestedly, 'You 'wake, Abby?'

And she was right side up again, because the only important thing in this huge mess was Michael. 'Yes, darling, I'm awake! What time is it?'

'Ha'-pas' four,' he said promptly and inaccurately, and ran across the room to give her a hug and good-morning kiss. Newly minted as the dawn, he was dressed in his favourite jeans and the sweatshirt with the dog on the front. 'Uncle Caelan says you can have breakfast in bed if you like.'

She most emphatically did *not* like. 'Tell him to give me ten minutes to wash my face and I'll join you both.'

Giggling, and clearly on the best of terms with the world, he left on a shout of, 'Uncle Caelan, Uncle Caelan, she's getting up!'

Exactly ten minutes later Abby walked into the room off the kitchen, to find Michael perched on a cushion on one of the dining chairs, his shiny face eager as he watched his uncle approach with a packet of cereal.

Caelan glanced at her astonished face. 'I found this in your emergency pack,' he said drily. 'Do you eat it too?'

Abby shook her head. Emotions tumbled around her mind in chaotic disarray, but of course Caelan was in full control. 'Toast, thank you,' she said.

He nodded at a bowl on the table, saying laconically, 'Stewed tamarillos. Help yourself,' as he poured cereal into the bowl in front of Michael.

Who warmed her heart by politely thanking his uncle as he picked up his spoon. Abby sat down, wondering if

Caelan had made sure there were tamarillos because his investigator had found out they were her favourite fruit.

Stop that right now, she commanded. Possibly she *had* told someone in Nukuroa that she loved tamarillos, but it meant nothing; part of the reason for Caelan's formidable success was a brain like a calculator.

He sat down and shot her an assessing look, his brows drawing together. 'I hope you slept well.'

Once she got to sleep she had, although she recalled waking several times in turmoil, her mind filled with images that brought sudden, shameful heat to her skin. 'Very well, thank you,' she told him, hoping that her tone was steady enough to hide her jumping pulse.

At least her hand didn't tremble when she helped herself to the ruby-coloured fruit.

'Coffee?' His voice was courteous.

A touch of hysteria tightened her nerves. He was being the perfect host, she thought feverishly, but at least he wasn't freezing the air around him with his special brand of killer contempt.

She responded in kind, and with Michael as buffer breakfast proceeded in a state of apparent civility, neither adult acknowledging the fierce undercurrents that ran through the calm, civilised, idiotic conversation.

Caelan said, 'This morning I'll lodge a notice of intended marriage with the registrar. I'll need some information from you.'

Panic clutched her throat, but some time during the long night she'd accepted that this was going to happen. Stiffly she gave him the data he needed, watching as he wrote it down with swift, slashing strokes of his pen.

'I'll organise the wedding,' he said, 'but you'll need to do some shopping. I'll pick you up at two this afternoon.' He made another note. 'I'll also organise an appointment with a solicitor so that you can go over a pre-nuptial agreement and the necessity for the adoption process.'

Astonished, she met his keen, impervious gaze. He waited, and when she said nothing he added quietly, 'Be here.'

Abby's head came up. She met his eyes with unflinching dignity. 'We both know,' she said, choosing her words with extreme care, 'that sooner or later there will be an opportunity for your—new housemates—to leave. Imprisonment isn't possible.'

His brows snapped together in a forbidding frown. 'Your point is?'

Abby quelled a nervous flutter. 'I've agreed to marry you. I won't go back on my word.'

Caelan's silence was a tangible force in the room, predatory, intimidating. He glanced at Michael, who was applying himself with gusto to the bowl of cereal.

His hard smile sent shivers of foreboding down her spine. 'Very well,' he said, and held out his hand. 'Shall we shake on it?'

Reluctantly she extended hers. 'Why would you trust a handshake?'

'I trust it about as much as I trust you, but it's the recognised thing,' he said.

His grip was firm and impersonal, but she shivered when she looked into his narrowed analytical eyes. She knew what he was doing—proving to her again that the raw physical magic was as strong as ever, that her body sang when she saw him because every cell in it recognised him.

White-lipped, she jerked her hand free.

And then Michael slipped down from his chair and stuck out his hand. Abby said nothing, watching as

Caelan stooped and took the small paw and shook it gently. Michael grinned. When Caelan smiled back something tight and hard and fiercely defended shattered inside Abby's heart.

'Very well,' Caelan said. 'It's a deal.'

With a final keen look, he turned and the door closed behind him. Abby drew a deep breath, feeling as though she'd just come battered and bloody through a battle.

'Come on, Michael,' she said cheerfully. 'Finish your breakfast. We've got things to do.'

In spite of the changes in their lives, she was going to make some sort of routine for him. And if she clung to the idea because she needed the reassurance of normality, then that was all right too.

CHAPTER SIX

ABBY had washed the dishes and made their beds when two women from the hotel housekeeping staff arrived to circumvent any further attempts at housekeeping. She and Michael unpacked his books and arranged them on the shelves in his bedroom. Later, she coaxed him into the saddle of the rocking-horse.

It didn't take him long to decide that this was a wonderful experience. Half an hour of vigorous riding followed by a running game on the terrace before lunch used up some of his boundless energy, but he needed more space. Tropically exuberant though the penthouse terrace was with its lush plants in huge pots and the view of the harbour—today a shimmering silver-blue expanse beneath a benign spring sky—he was accustomed to an expanse of lawn with trees to climb.

Shortly after midday the housekeeping staff departed, leaving the apartment immaculate. Abby made lunch, Michael demolished it with gusto, then yawned widely.

'I'm not tired,' he maintained stoutly.

'Of course you are,' Abby said, scooping him up and hugging him. 'And the sooner you have your nap, the sooner Uncle Caelan will be here!'

Much struck by this, he went to bed with an eagerness that roused a simmer of jealousy in her.

She bent to kiss him softly on his cheek, but outside his room she hesitated, wondering how to fill in the next hour. Since she'd brought Michael to New Zealand, she'd been so busy she'd had little time for introspection; work and caring for him had taken every ounce of energy she possessed.

She'd longed for time to read, to garden, to go to a movie.

Now she had no work and too much time to think— thoughts she didn't want to face, intensified by long-repressed emotions.

Tensely she walked out into the warm, fresh air. The penthouse unnerved her, so superbly decorated she didn't dare let Michael go anywhere but the casual dining and living area off the kitchen. How on earth were they going to deal with a palace, if that was what they were going to stay in on Dacia?

Bumble-bees colliding in her stomach, she recalled the rented house in Nukuroa, sparse and bare, its bedrooms faintly smelling of mould in spite of everything she could do, the elderly stove with chipped enamel and electric elements that wobbled whenever she put a saucepan on them…

She'd worried about Michael's health in that house, longed for the money to rent somewhere better. Yet now, lapped in luxury, she thought with a wry, painful grimace that if she could click her heels together and find herself back there she'd never ask for anything again.

And if the apartment intimidated her, how was she going to cope with Dacia and its royal family?

Or—the big one—with life as Caelan's wife?

Heat flared suddenly inside her, sweet and fierce and heady. He meant to have her, and she, pitifully weak where he was concerned, would fight him as best she could, but in the end she'd give in.

How could she bear that—to give everything she had and always be aware that it meant nothing to him beyond the transient satisfaction of an animal appetite?

Caelan strode silently out through the glass doors. His hooded gaze sought Abby, and found her, slender—too slender, he thought on a spurt of irrational anger—examining one of the large potted palms.

She had her back to him, a T-shirt in just the wrong shade of green skimming trousers cut for a more matronly figure than hers. Only her feet, slimly elegant in a pair of cheap sandals, reminded him of the woman he'd once kissed because he couldn't help himself.

But nothing could take away from her natural grace. Or his reaction to it; at the sight of her his body sprang to life, desire summoned by a primal hunger he'd never experienced with any other woman.

What was it about her that snapped the leash on his control? He'd always enjoyed sophisticated, intelligent lovers, women who were self-sufficient and confident. Although Abby was intelligent, her actions spoke of a life ruled by impulse and emotions—the sort of woman he'd consciously avoided because they'd have demanded too much from him.

No wonder she and Gemma had become friends.

Grief caught him unawares, mingled as always with anger and a gnawing conviction of failure. If he'd been available to his sister when she'd discovered her pregnancy he'd have been able to keep her safe.

But she'd gone to Abby, and to a death that need never have happened.

Abby stirred, the sun lighting up her hair in a tongue of fire. Ignoring a fierce jab of satisfaction because she'd washed most of that damned colouring out of it, he started towards her.

He hadn't taken more than a couple of steps when her spine stiffened. She didn't move, didn't turn her head, but he knew she'd sensed his presence.

Damn her, he thought with unusual anger, for once she could acknowledge him! He stopped behind her, waiting until she turned her head.

'Oh, hello,' she said warily, her features so composed he knew she'd been practising. 'Did you have a good morning?'

'You sound very wifely,' he said, not hiding the irony in his tone. 'Yes, the morning went well. How was yours?'

'So far, so good.' But a little frown furrowed her delicate brows and she returned her gaze to the feathery fronds of the palm tree as though finding enlightenment there. 'Michael's still asleep. I hope you're not planning to wake him up.'

'Why would I do that?'

She gave a short shrug. 'To fit him into your busy schedule.'

He said coolly, 'I plan to be around for Michael whenever he needs me.' And before she had a chance to say anything he added, 'We'll buy clothes for him this afternoon.' He scrutinised her with a cool smile before adding, 'One of Auckland's best salons is holding a showing for you tomorrow morning. The wedding's organised for three days' time, and we fly out to Dacia immediately afterwards.'

She opened her mouth to reply somewhat heatedly to his high-handed authority, only to be cut off by the imperative summons of a telephone.

'I'm sorry,' he said abruptly, taking a small mobile phone from his pocket. 'This must be important.' He walked away, not speaking until he was out of hearing range.

Jealousy, bitter and dark, sliced through her. Although she couldn't hear what he said a subliminal instinct told her he was talking to a woman. Outrage clawed across her heart; she swung abruptly around and started for her bedroom.

'Abby,' Michael announced accusingly from his doorway, 'I'm awake. You said Uncle Caelan would be here soon!'

She forced a tender smile; his sunny nature took a few minutes to reassert itself after sleep. 'He's talking on his phone out on the terrace. Let's go and wash your face.'

How could she expect Caelan to trust her if she didn't extend him the same courtesy? He'd told her he intended being faithful; for her own peace of mind, she had to believe him. So she plucked the poisoned dart of jealousy from her mind and tried not to wonder if this promised faithfulness started on the wedding day or before…

Michael looked past her, his face lighting up. 'I want Uncle Caelan to wash my face,' he announced.

'Then you'd better ask him politely,' Abby suggested.

He thrust out his lower lip and looked sideways at her. 'You ask him, Abby.'

'Ask him what?' Caelan said from behind her.

Michael, stumbling a little, lifted his face and asked him.

Struck again by that fleeting resemblance between them, Abby drew in a sharp breath. Except for his brilliant eyes Caelan was a study in darkness—Mediterranean black hair, midnight brows and lashes, warm olive-bronze skin—while Michael's colouring bathed him in sunlight, yet they shared the same strong bone structure and arrogant nose.

Caelan's deep voice broke into her thoughts. 'Anything you need to tell me about this face-washing?'

She forced a smile and a light tone. 'Michael knows what to do.'

They came back five minutes later, Michael damp around the hairline and excited. 'Abby, Uncle Caelan says when I can swim properly he'll take me out in his boat!'

'Then you'll have to try really hard, won't you?' Abby said cheerfully. Was Caelan making sure she realised the difference his presence in Michael's life would make?

Caelan said, 'He already has the basics, and there's an excellent swimming school for pre-schoolers in Auckland.'

She nodded. Swimming, rocking horses, new clothes and new books were important, she decided sombrely as they went down in the lift, but more was needed to make a happy child. Although Gemma had grown up in a home where wealth was taken for granted, it hadn't brought her serenity or confidence. The only way Caelan could become important to Gemma's son was to give him time and affection.

It did seem that he was prepared to do that for Michael, but time would tell. Parenting success depended on the long haul, not short sprints.

Michael chattered non-stop about swimming all the way to one of the northern suburbs. Inside the shop however, he fell silent, gazing around with awed delight.

After a startled survey, Abby said wryly, 'This looks more like a coral reef than a children's clothes shop—sheer tots' heaven. How did you find out about this place?'

Caelan looked down at her with sardonic eyes. 'The owner contacted me for help; she had a vision, but couldn't get anyone to back her in it.'

One of his lovers? 'I'll bet it's doing well,' Abby observed tightly.

'She's worked hard; she deserves her success.' He

changed the subject without finesse. 'I suggest you choose clothes suitable for travelling. It will still be warm in Dacia when we arrive, so he'll need gear for playing outdoors and going to the beach, as well as some more formal outfits for meeting the relatives.'

For once, Michael didn't wriggle when it came to trying on clothes, and, with the help of a young assistant who knew exactly how to head off imminent boredom, they managed to acquire a wardrobe for him with the minimum amount of fuss.

What surprised Abby most was Caelan's attitude. It should have warmed her heart that, sophisticated and cynical though he was, he seemed to enjoy Michael's company. Instead, she felt as though she were on a slippery slope to some menace she couldn't discern.

And even relief at not being forced to squeeze every cent until it shrieked didn't overcome that unease.

Outside the shop Caelan said calmly, 'I'll take Michael home while you see the solicitor.'

His unreadable gaze lingered a moment on her bright hair. A shock of excitement sizzled through her like electricity.

But beneath that purely physical reaction lurked the formless fear that he might whisk Michael away so she'd never see him again. She looked up, flushing when she saw his mocking smile. He knew what she was thinking.

It was ridiculous to let the same old fears surface over and over again. Caelan had made it clear that he saw her and Michael as a package, and she suspected that he was learning to like his nephew. He must realise that Michael needed her.

'All right,' she said distantly, irritated because he was taking over again.

Middle-aged and efficient, the solicitor talked over the

pre-nuptial agreement that set out what Caelan expected of her as Michael's mother and his wife. She pointed out several areas that Abby should consider before she signed it, while saying that it seemed to protect both her and Michael's rights as well as the legal system could.

'Of course, the simplest way to safeguard the child's future,' she said, 'is for you both to adopt him. Has the prince—Mr Bagaton—discussed this with you?'

'Yes. It seems a good idea.'

'It will certainly give him legal standing as your child.'

Abby asked tightly, 'I assume that a stable marriage is important in the adoption process.'

After a keen glance, the solicitor said simply, 'Very.'

Back in the penthouse Michael was bursting with excitement; while they'd been away a splendid children's gym had been delivered and assembled on the terrace. 'Look at me, look at me, Abby,' he shouted, hanging by his knees from a bar. 'There's a slide here too!'

Acutely aware of Caelan's scrutiny, she exclaimed over its beauty and multitude of features. Finally she said, 'Did you thank Uncle Caelan for buying it for you?'

Michael scrambled off and stared at him. 'He didn't say,' he muttered. He gave his uncle a charming, lopsided grin. 'Thank you, Uncle Caelan!'

'I'm glad you like it,' Caelan told him. But when Michael had run back to his new toy, he said, 'I don't want his thanks.'

Abby turned baffled eyes onto his hard face. 'Why?'

He gave her a long, measuring look, then shrugged. 'Gemma once said that I tried to buy her affection. It wasn't true, but I don't think it would be good for Michael to feel that all good things come from me.'

Surprised, she said, 'That's—very thoughtful of you.

But saying thank you is a necessary part of bringing up a child.'

Something happened between them, some sort of communication deeper than words. She felt her skin tighten and swallowed to ease a dry throat. 'I'd better unpack his new clothes.'

Caelan stopped her with a hand on her arm. She froze, and humiliating excitement leapt into full life.

Dropping his hand, he said, 'What did you think of the pre-nuptial agreement?'

'It seemed very fair.'

He was watching her too closely. Something swift and impetuous scudded the length of her spine, and her breath came too fast.

'In that case we can sign it tomorrow morning before we go shopping. I've opened a bank account for you.'

When she opened her mouth to protest he put a lean forefinger over her lips. Her mouth dried and she stared into eyes as cool and enigmatic as the sea, the blue irises edged by a silver-grey band that gave them their distinctive translucence.

Coolly unyielding, he said, 'I don't want to hear any futile objections. You read the agreement—the allowance is specified there. If it's not enough, we can adjust it later.'

He removed his finger and Abby could breathe again. Feeling in some obscure way as though she was compromising her integrity, she said colourlessly, 'All right.' And vowed to spend as little of his money as she could.

Amusement gleamed in the depths of his eyes. 'I suggest that instead of looking for an excuse to fight—or kiss—we consider Michael's welfare and keep our more volatile reactions under strict discipline.'

Skin heating, Abby ignored the beginning of that sentence. 'Yes,' she returned with spurious sweetness, 'let's just do that.'

That night after dinner Caelan said abruptly, 'Tell me about Gemma.'

Abby put her cup of coffee onto the table beside her chair. Feeling her way cautiously, she asked, 'What about her?'

'Why did she leave her mother's house to go to Palaweyo? She must have known it was no place for her to have a child.'

Abby chose her words carefully. 'She didn't know she was pregnant when she arrived; she'd come to think things over, she said.'

'What things?'

'Whether or not to marry Mike.'

He looked surprised. 'I didn't realise it had gone so far.'

Abby said quietly, 'She'd only been there a week when Mike called, telling her about the rescue. She pleaded with him not to do it, but he told her he had to and that he loved her. Then we heard of his death. I was so worried—she went all silent and distant, as though to get the courage to keep going she had to call on all her reserves.'

He said harshly, 'You should have got in touch with me.'

'I wanted her to call you.' Abby couldn't look at him; guilt still cast its dark pall over her. If she'd given in to the temptation to go behind Gemma's back and call Caelan, his sister would still be alive. 'She said she'd run to you for every little thing in her life, and that now she had to deal with this by herself.'

He said something under his breath and she flinched.

'Caelan, I'm so sorry.'

'It wasn't your fault,' he said evenly. 'Yes, I'd have liked you to contact me, but she was an adult and your friend. It would have been a betrayal.'

Incredibly relieved, Abby swallowed to ease a dry throat. 'When she found out she was pregnant it seemed to give her the courage to keep going. I insisted she get the doctor at the hospital to check her out. He said she was fine, so I thought it was safe to let her stay.'

Caelan said harshly, 'I wish I'd known.'

'Gemma said you were under tremendous pressure with a really bad problem in some part of the corporation.'

Abby thought she'd strained every bit of condemnation from her voice, but he glanced at her as though she'd directly accused him. 'A rogue manager in South America was siphoning off funds to acquire his own cocaine enterprise; he had links to a terrorist cell. Several of my people were kidnapped by them, a couple killed. It took time and effort to lure them out of the jungle and into custody, but if I'd known Gemma needed me I'd have been there for her.'

Abby believed him. 'She knew that. And she achieved some sort of peace in Palaweyo, even while she grieved for Mike. I wouldn't say she was happy, but she managed a sort of quiet contentment. And when his son was born she was—awed, and stunned at how much she loved him, how hugely important he was to her, how he changed everything. She'd started talking about taking him back to New Zealand when the cyclone struck.'

'I'm glad of that,' he said, his voice cold and detached.

But something glittered in his pale eyes, and Abby's heart was wrung. Without thinking she got up and went over, putting her hand on his arm and looking up into a face as cold as flint. Urgently, wanting only to offer comfort, she said, 'She didn't die in pain, Caelan. She said that Mike was waiting for her, and she kissed Michael goodbye and she was smiling when she died—so peacefully.'

With an odd raw sound deep in his throat, Caelan pulled her into his arms. They contracted around her and his mouth came down on hers, famished and avid.

Although Abby fought the surge of passionate abandon, trying to force her body into passive stillness, it was no use. A tide of white-hot sensation swamped caution, washing it away into regions beyond recovery, along with her will-power and her common sense.

She swayed and linked her hands around Caelan's neck, fingertips thrilling to the texture of his dark hair, warm from his powerful body.

Their hungry kisses—deep as those of lovers reunited after an eternity of loneliness—broke down every barrier. And when he said her name against her lips, the primal note of possession in his voice released the shackles around her heart.

She wanted Caelan; she had to accept that she always would. And he wanted her. That elemental sorcery still linked them with chains of desire and need.

Elation and despair melded in bittersweet response; in his arms, with his kisses on her lips, she felt reborn, even though nothing had changed.

But when he cupped the soft curve of her breast, she froze, jerked back into reality by the keen, exquisite pang of delight that arrowed from his hand to the place that longed to welcome him in the most intimate of all embraces.

If she let this happen, she'd not only experience the glory of sexual awakening but the pain and the eventual despair. This man, she thought desperately, is forcing you into a marriage you don't want.

The only barrier left was her self-respect.

'No!' The word was torn from her, guttural with intense emotion. She couldn't let this go further; it would kill her to become his toy, his mistress-wife.

Cold satisfaction glittered in Caelan's hooded eyes.

'Why not?' His voice came deep and raw and demanding through lips that barely moved. Warm and sure and confident, his thumb moved back and forth across the pleading tip of her breast.

Despising herself for the rills of unbearable pleasure coursing through her, she said aggressively, 'Because I don't want it.'

The perfect opening, she realised the moment the words left her mouth, and cursed herself for handing it to him.

His mouth hardened into a mirthless smile. 'When your actions speak as loudly as your words, I might believe you.'

'Believe me now,' she said bleakly, adding with stark, sharp honesty, 'My body appears to be beyond my control, but my head and my heart don't want it.'

He looked into her eyes with piercing intentness; she held her breath and met that probing stare with defiance.

Finally, he let her go.

Shivering, her mind so tumultuous she didn't know what she was thinking, she watched him walk across to the balustrade. That long, silent stride, his lethal male grace, the sheer masculine presence of the man summoned a vivid, blinding image from out of nowhere.

Caelan with his knees clamped around the barrel of a rearing horse, long hair flying in some long-dead wind, a sword in his hand, eyes gleaming with cold determi-

nation and a ferocious battle cry on his lips as he reached down for her...

Blinking, she swallowed and the swift vision snapped out, banished by the taunt in his voice when he swung around and said, 'Want it or not, Abby—and you can't despise this embarrassing hunger more than I do—it's not going to go away.'

'We don't have to act on it,' she returned with curt emphasis. 'It's only lust—and lust dies if it's not satisfied.'

He lifted a satirical eyebrow. 'Four years without satisfaction doesn't seem to have quenched it.'

Did he mean that he'd—? No!

One glance at his lean, arrogant face scotched that thought. Of course he hadn't been celibate since that first kiss! She knew of at least two lovers in the intervening years.

Those kisses had been a test. If she'd given in he'd have taken her, without emotion, without compassion.

Her emotions churned in wild disarray, while her body simmered with resentful disappointment at being deprived of his love-making. Abruptly, unable to bear being in the same room as him, she said, 'I meant what I said.'

Handsome face cast from bronze, he said mockingly, 'Ah, yes, but how long do you think you can fight it?'

Willing her composure to hold for a few minutes longer, she retorted with passion, 'I won't be a convenient outlet to be used whenever it suits you. This isn't going to work unless you understand that.' His cynical smile goaded her over the edge. Rashly she finished, 'If you can't keep your hands to yourself, then I'll leave and take Michael with me.'

He leaned back against the balustrade, narrow hips emphasising his long legs and wide shoulders. 'Do that,' he said, his gaze burning like ice and a white line around his mouth, 'and I'll hunt you down—right across the world if I have to.'

He paused a taut, terrifying second before adding with silky precision, 'And when I find you, you'll wish I hadn't.'

She hoped her involuntary shudder didn't register with him. 'I don't mean that I'd run away again.'

'Then what *did* you mean?' He didn't wait for an answer. 'Forget this idea of living somewhere in Auckland and granting me visitation rights. I won't be a part-time presence in Michael's life. He's had too many of those already. And I don't trust you. You kidnapped him once.'

Heatedly she returned, 'Only because I knew you'd take him away from me. You would have, wouldn't you?'

He didn't answer straight away. The silence loomed, almost threatening, until he said, 'Surely Gemma must have known that I'd do my best for him.'

Was there a note of pain beneath the level words? Abby said quietly, 'Of course she did.'

Caelan swung on his heel to stare out across the lights and the harbour. Something about the stiffness of his shoulders persuaded her to continue tentatively. 'She loved you, Caelan, and respected you, but she knew how busy you were. And you've already admitted that her childhood was lonely.'

He shrugged, dismissing the subject. 'This isn't getting us anywhere, and we've got no time to hash over things we can't change. My cousin Luka has suggested that you might like to choose an emerald from the Dacian collection for an engagement ring, but if you'd rather have anything else we can organise that.'

Engagement ring? Her stomach contracted as though warding off a blow. 'I haven't thought of it.'

'You'll need one. A notice announcing our engagement will be issued once we're in Dacia, and official photographs will be released. I'd prefer it if you don't mention the first ceremony, as it's just to set the wheels of the social welfare system on track here. Any indication could attract media attention.'

'I see,' she said colourlessly, inwardly appalled at the prospect of reporters and photographers lurking in ambush. 'I don't know about the ring—what do you think would be best?'

He shrugged. 'We'll take Luka up on his offer. There's bound to be an emerald in the treasury that matches your eyes. I have an early appointment tomorrow, but I'll pick you up around ten.'

'What for?'

'You're buying clothes.'

Abby had forgotten completely about the private showing at the salon. She opened her mouth to protest, then closed it. Although she was intensely reluctant to admit it, she craved the armour of clothes that at least fitted her, in colours that suited her.

'All right,' she said reluctantly.

He smiled and came across the room to stand in front of her. He startled her by touching the soft crease where her lips curved. 'I like your smile,' he said softly, and before she could stop him he kissed the corner of her mouth.

Traitor that it was, her body responded with blatant delight. She had to clench her fists to stop herself from inhaling his scent, faint and entirely male, so erotic it melted her bones and sent her blood racing through her body.

'Dream of that,' he said, his voice rough and urgent. 'For whatever satisfaction dreams give you.'

CHAPTER SEVEN

THREE days later at the beach house, Abby sucked in her breath and stared at herself in a mirror. A woman she didn't recognise gazed back at her from wide, glittery green eyes. She looked feverish—the glow in her skin so hectic that her brand-new, expensive cosmetics barely toned it down, and lips riper and fuller and more obvious than ever.

The tawny gold of the slender silk suit only added to that betraying air of lush anticipation. In the frighteningly exclusive salon in Auckland it had looked restrained and sophisticated, the short sleeves and wide, scooped neckline vaguely bridal without implying that sort of hopeful, happy delight that should be symbolic of marriage.

Not this marriage; it was a mockery, and she didn't want Caelan to think she was going into it with expectations he couldn't fulfil.

She adjusted the top, moving slightly so that sunlight tangled golden in the crystal embroidery of the jacket, beneath which she wore a bra made of satin and lace and a whisper-soft camisole the same colour as the suit.

Caelan—or his PA—had organised a trip to an incredibly chic salon where her hair had been washed, conditioned and styled into a sleek cut that restored the sheen.

Despairing, because the loose waves added to that eagerly expectant look, she picked up a comb and ruthlessly pulled it into a knot behind her head.

'I should have bought a veil to hide behind,' she muttered when it was done.

Of course she wore no engagement ring, and had no idea what wedding rings Caelan had chosen.

In fact, she thought bleakly, she didn't even know who the witnesses were! The helicopter pilot and the housekeeper, probably, or the hotel nanny who'd agreed to spend the weekend looking after Michael at one end of the beach house, while Abby and her new husband supposedly enjoyed a one-night honeymoon in the owner's suite at the other end.

Except that after the deed was done Abby would be spending the night in this guest bedroom, close enough to Caelan's to quieten any gossip. An aching sorrow welled up inside her and to her horror she had to blink back stinging tears.

It was no use crying for the moon; not in a million years would he have fallen in love with her.

This was for Michael, she reminded herself stringently.

She swung around at a knock on the door. 'Come in,' she called, her heart hammering madly against her ribs.

Neither the nanny nor the housekeeper came in. Tall, slim and darkly elegant, with a serene, aristocratic beauty, the woman who entered was a complete stranger, although her face seemed familiar. Her superb clothes indicated that she was also a wedding guest.

Feeling an utter fool, Abby stared blankly at her.

'I've just found out from Caelan that he didn't tell you we were coming,' the newcomer said severely. 'I love him very much, so I hate to think that he's too ashamed of us to even mention us! I am Lucia Radcliffe, his cousin, and my husband Hunt is busy pouring him a pre-wedding drink.'

Abby found her voice and said with banal formality, 'I—how do you do? I'm so glad you've come.'

And if Caelan was ashamed, it certainly wasn't of his lovely cousin!

Princess Lucia—whose name and face she recognised because they'd been scattered through magazines since her marriage a couple of years previously—smiled and closed the door behind her.

'And I am very glad to be here. You look absolutely exquisite, Abby.' She gave a mischievous smile. 'I always knew there was someone like you in Caelan's past.'

Abby swallowed. 'I'm not sure what you mean.'

The gleam of mischief deepened. 'I've never seen my darling cousin stressed enough to rely on whisky to restore his famous composure! He's the most maddening man—he knows exactly what he wants, and he's always so sure he'll get it. I used to long for the day when he'd meet someone who turned him inside out. And now I can see that he has. Ah, here comes the champagne!'

The housekeeper, looking flustered, entered carrying a tray with two crystal flutes and a bottle of what, Abby realised, was vintage wine.

'It'll steady your nerves,' the amazingly obtuse Princess Lucia said. 'Just take a couple of mouthfuls. Now, where are the flowers? Ah, yes, there they are.' She picked up the three magnificent tawny roses, and sniffed pleasurably. 'Gorgeous, aren't they? Little Michael is almost beside himself with anticipation, so take a second sip of wine and then let's go.'

Filling the silence with a stream of comforting chatter that somehow calmed Abby's fears, she got them out of the sanctuary of the bedroom and onto a wide terrace overlooking the white beach and the blue-green sea. Heavily wooded headlands sheltered the house and the bay from the ocean.

Closer at hand a temporary altar had been erected at

one end of the terrace, shaded from the bright sun by a white awning.

More stupid, swift tears stung Abby's eyes; she'd had no idea that Caelan had planned to go to such lengths—even to choosing roses that matched the ones she held.

Her eyes flew to him, tall and superbly confident by the altar. He dwarfed the glorious scenery and the superb house, dominating it more with his powerful personal magnetism than his impressive height. The exquisite tailoring of his business suit couldn't conceal the raw, primal power of the man; he looked exactly what he was, she thought with a swift skip of her heart—the leading male in the pride, the alpha lion.

Whenever she was with Caelan the world seemed a richer, more vibrant place.

Beside him stood another man, every bit as tall, the sun picking up highlights in his dark hair, his face lean and tough. Hunt Radcliffe, no doubt.

Michael was standing on Caelan's other side, one small hand clasped in his, his face serious.

The celebrant looked up as she and the princess came out, and everyone turned. Abby's heart jumped; Caelan smiled, and for a second she thought she saw something more than swift lust in his eyes.

Desire is a drug, she told herself sturdily. She'd always hoped that one day she'd find a man to love, yet, although she'd met some nice men over the past years, not one had stirred her blood.

In a sudden, unwilling leap of insight, she acknowledged that Caelan was the man who gave her life savour and meaning, the only man she'd ever really wanted—the only she'd ever want.

Enter heartbreak, stage left, she thought with bleak desperation.

She met his eyes with a hint of defiance, stunned when he smiled at her, a lazy movement of his mouth that reminded her too vividly of his kisses.

'Abby,' he said deeply, and strode to meet her as though she was the most precious thing in his life.

He didn't touch her, but he didn't need to; he'd stamped his possession of her as clearly as if he'd swept her off her feet and kissed her.

And some primitive part of her rejoiced, even though it was a bitter farce played for the benefit of anyone who happened to be watching.

Michael said in an awestruck voice, 'Abby, you look jus' like the princess in my book!'

And everyone smiled. Swallowing, Abby went with Caelan up to the table that served as an altar. Lucia Radcliffe moved to stand by her husband, and Caelan slid his free hand around Abby's, holding it in a warm, strong grip while he reached for Michael's little paw with his other. Linked as the family they would be from now on, he and Michael and Abby went through the brief, unbearably moving ceremony.

Although her hand trembled when they exchanged wedding rings—identical bands of gold—she at last felt a kind of acceptance. It might not be the marriage she had longed for, but it would make Michael safe, and she'd find what comfort she could in that.

'You may kiss the bride,' the celebrant said.

Abby tensed. She didn't expect Caelan to kiss her with any sort of passion, but she was surprised when he stooped and picked up Michael before dropping a brief kiss on her lips. Michael hugged her and kissed her, burrowing his head into her shoulder, and then lifted his face and kissed Caelan on his cheek.

Caelan's face softened miraculously. It would be worth it, Abby repeated. It had to be…

Princess Lucia kissed her on the cheek. 'Welcome, dear Abby, to our family,' she said with every appearance of pleasure.

Hunt Radcliffe lifted her hand and dropped a kiss on the back of it. 'You'll get used to it,' he said cheerfully, watching her with cool, shrewd midnight-blue eyes. 'And once the official hullabaloo in Dacia is over, you can flee back to New Zealand where you won't have to deal with all that dull official protocol.'

His wife snorted in a most unladylike way. 'Don't listen to him, Abby—there's nothing to worry about.' Tawny eyes smiling at her husband, she added, 'Any time protocol reared its ugly head, Hunt dealt with it, and you will too.'

Although her husband's lean face gave little away, Abby sensed the strong, fierce love that linked them. A wave of bitter envy shocked her.

She wanted desperately to ask about the ceremony in Dacia, but it wasn't the time—her question would give too much away about their relationship. Clearly Caelan hadn't told his cousin and her husband why they were marrying; she didn't dare compromise the secret.

At all costs they had to behave like people in love, determined to make a good marriage that would last—at least until Michael grew up.

So when Caelan curved his arm around her, she leaned into his shoulder and tried to summon a radiant smile while the two men shook hands.

'Protocol isn't the sort of thing you have to worry about when you're growing up in a citrus orchard,' she said, while her body thrummed with delight at the strength that held her so lightly. He smelt so *good*, she thought, and flushed when she saw the princess's eyes twinkle.

But the other woman said calmly, 'It's not some deep, dark mystery; it's easy enough to learn—look at Alexa. She comes from a typical New Zealand background, and the Dacians adore her because she's everything a ruling princess should be, warm and gracious and deeply interested in them.' She flashed a reassuring smile at Abby. 'If you can seat a dinner party you'll do fine. And Caelan will help—he's an expert.'

Grateful to her for her attempt to give her confidence, Abby said, 'I know he will.'

Deep and completely confident, Caelan's voice reverberated through his chest, sending little shivers of pleasure through her. 'Abby won't have any difficulty,' he said. 'Now, how about some champagne?'

Looking back, Abby realised that he stage-managed the hour after the ceremony with consummate skill. They drank a glass of wine with the celebrant and the housekeeper and nanny, then the nanny whisked Michael off to their end of the house, and the helicopter removed the celebrant to the mainland. A delicious dinner was served on the terrace as the sun sank slowly, its fading brilliance casting a beguiling cloak of witchery and glamour over the bay.

Abby decided she liked cool, tough Hunt Radcliffe and his princess, especially when his wife produced photographs of her gorgeous little daughter.

'As her godfather,' she informed Caelan, 'you'll be interested to know that she now has four very sharp little teeth, but no sign of any others. And she adores blueberries.'

To Abby's surprise Caelan admired the photographs,

and from the subsequent conversation it was clear that he saw a lot of little Natalia Radcliffe.

Although Gemma had talked about her brother, she'd barely scratched the surface of his complex and intriguing character.

Hunt and Lucia—whom Caelan called Cia—left after dinner as the sun was setting. Watching the helicopter head straight into the glory of gold and apricot to the west, she said, 'Does everyone in your family fly their own private helicopter?'

'Quite a few,' he said calmly. 'You'll get used to it.'

It didn't seem likely. Trying to hide her stretched nerves with a calm, brisk tone, she said, 'I'll go and check on Michael.'

Caelan turned his head and surveyed her. What was she thinking? It was impossible to tell; her face was half turned away from him, but for all this interminable day her expression had been controlled and self-contained, the long, thick lashes over her almond-shaped eyes successfully hiding her emotions.

Quelling an undisciplined urge to smash through that self-contained barrier, he said, 'We'll both go.'

She stiffened, before saying colourlessly, 'Yes, of course.'

At first she'd resisted the idea of hiring the nanny to accompany them, but he'd insisted. While she'd chosen her wardrobe at the exclusive showing in the salon, Michael had been enjoying his stint in the hotel nursery with the friendly middle-aged woman, and had greeted her this morning with every appearance of pleasure.

It irritated Caelan that he still wasn't sure why he'd been so determined that the nanny should come. As they walked through the house, fragrant with the scent of the sea and the balsam of feathery kanuka trees, he accepted grimly that each day they spent together made him more aware of his wife.

His wife. A surge of elemental possessiveness startled him. So damned elusive, with the face of a sexy faerie woman and her slender, sensuous body, but he thought he was beginning to discern the lights and shadows of her personality. She kept her promises, at no matter what cost to herself. She loved Michael with the fierce, self-sacrificing adoration of a mother. She'd coped with Lucia and Hunt, and he'd been pleased by the way she took over the reins of the evening, sliding unconsciously into the role of hostess. Although he suspected she didn't realise it, she had a deep inner confidence that probably came from that life as the loved only child of two happy parents.

And she couldn't hide the fact that, although she resented the way he'd dragooned her into this marriage, she wanted him, he thought with a fierce, shockingly primitive satisfaction.

Michael was sound asleep. Abby kissed the boy's satiny cheek and watched as Caelan did the same.

On the way back, she asked something that had been bothering her. 'Do Lucia and Hunt know about Michael's parentage?'

'Yes, of course, but they don't know about the arrangement we have come to. They think we are marrying for real,' he said coolly.

Abby stared at his hard face, the afterglow emphasising lines and planes sculpted by authority and a formidable will. That primal anticipation stirred within her, flexing claws.

Abby thought of Hunt Radcliffe, whose shrewd eyes had been backed by his intelligent conversation, and his wife, carefully not asking any questions. 'Do you really think they believe that?' she asked baldly.

'I don't care whether they do or not.' His voice took on an inflexible edge. 'I'm sure you'll agree that the fewer people who know that you lied to get Michael out of Palaweyo, the better.'

'Yes,' she admitted bleakly. 'Does *anyone* in your family know the real situation?'

'No. And if they have any inkling that all is not quite as straightforward as it seems, they'll keep quiet. We do secrets rather well in our family.' He dismissed the subject with a shrug. 'Don't worry, Abby.'

It said a lot for the effect he had on her, she thought warily, that she'd only just realised something he seemed to have missed. 'What if the writer you told me about— the one who's researching a book about Palaweyo—finds out?'

'I'll buy him off,' he said coolly. 'Yes, you can curl your lip, but most people have an asking price.'

Some note in his voice made her look up sharply. Was he implying that she'd married him for his money? His handsome face gave nothing away, and the ice-blue eyes were cool and translucent and completely unreadable.

By then they'd arrived back on the terrace. From somewhere inside came the low sound of music, and a glow in the east promised a moon. Caelan said abruptly, 'Would you like to dance?'

'What?' But her blood was picking up speed and her limbs felt weighted with sweet languor.

'It seems a pity to waste the music and the night, and the moon.' He held out his arm, and, although she knew she was dicing with danger, she placed the tips of her fingers on it, every sense taut with a feverish, forbidden anticipation.

His eyes gleamed in the gathering darkness, and when she moved into his embrace he steered her out of the light and into the shadows on the edge of the terrace, where a massive pohutukawa tree leaned over the railing. When summer came it would be blood-red with its strange, tasselled flowers...

The sultry, seductive singer's plaint wove a smoky veil of love lost and regretted. It hit too close to the bone. Too wary to relax, alarmed by the way her skin seemed to have thinned, Abby held herself stiffly.

Of course he was a terrific dancer. Their steps matched perfectly, so she willed herself to relax and enjoy this rare moment of peace in his arms.

Not that the peace lasted long. Too soon it was replaced by an insidious passion, a slow fever in the blood that blotted out everything but his presence, his touch on her hand, the faint, erotic fragrance that was his alone— male magnetism incarnate.

She bent her head so that he couldn't see her face, but that brought her forehead too close to his broad chest, and she had to fight the need to lean against him and let him take her wherever he wanted to.

The music slowed. Turning, he drew her closer with a strong arm across her back, and the simmering heat leaped into full blaze when she felt the strength of his thighs against hers and realised that he was aroused.

So was she, she thought with odd elation. These past few days had honed the forbidden attraction into mindless need, and if he wanted to take her to bed tonight she'd go with him, because hunger had eaten away her defences. The only concession she'd make to pride was not to suggest it herself, and that was getting harder by the minute.

He said quietly above her head, 'Relax. The worst is

over; tomorrow we'll sign the papers and have the first interview with the social worker assigned to our case. And once we get to Dacia you'll be fine; Michael will have little relatives to play with, and Cia and Hunt are familiar faces to you now.'

Another wedding, more princes and princesses, a life totally alien to anything she'd ever known. After a shallow breath Abby said tonelessly, 'Is that why you asked them here?'

His mouth curved in an enigmatic smile. 'To an extent—but I'm also dynastic enough to want some family at both our weddings.'

She straightened her shoulders. 'I'll make mistakes— I just hope they won't be glaring ones.'

'If you make mistakes,' he said coolly, the faint foreign intonation she'd noticed in his voice intensifying, 'it will be my fault for not taking care of you. Don't worry; my entire family are looking forward to meeting you, and, after your brilliant impersonation of a woman in love, Cia will tell them you hold my heart in your hand. As they've mostly succumbed to love, they'll be delighted to see someone else caught in its snare.'

His light, mocking tone hurt. And he was right—love was a snare, a dangerous, intoxicating blend of need and desire and the urge to give, all wrapped up in seductive hope and tied with the glorious promise of happiness.

If only we'd had time, she thought, and promptly chided herself for being so stupid. After all, Caelan had made a sacrifice too; instead of marrying a woman from his own world, a sophisticated, elegant woman who knew how to behave and what to say and the right sort of clothes to wear, he'd tied himself in marriage to a woman he despised.

For Michael.

Fighting back a swift, sharp ache of pain, she said brightly, 'I like your cousin. She's very kind.'

'She's a good woman,' he returned, easing her a little closer to his lean, strong body. 'She doesn't suffer fools gladly, but she's met her match in Hunt. Of course he's as besotted with her as she is with him, so they're happy.'

He sounded amused, as though he couldn't imagine what it would be like to love a woman as much as Hunt loved his wife.

Abby said, 'Their daughter sounds adorable.'

He laughed. 'She's a small package of charm hiding an implacable will. God help the world when she grows up!'

His arm tightened across her back. The music had sunk to a smoky, intensely personal whisper, backed by the ageless hush of the small waves on the beach. Every sense screwed to a pitch of intensity, Abby thought that she'd never forget these minutes spent in his arms. The singer's sultry voice lamenting a lost love, the subtle scent of salt mingling with the faint male essence that was Caelan's alone, the warmth of his hard body blasting through the silk that caressed her skin—all combined to release the lock she'd kept on her inhibitions.

Tonight, she thought dreamily, closing her eyes and resting her cheek lightly against the smooth material of his coat, she'd do what she wanted without thinking of anything but her own pleasure...

And Caelan's. Strange that after deciding as an adolescent that she'd wait for the sort of love her parents had before she committed herself to any man, she should fall for a man with a pirate's attitude towards life.

Except that they did have things in common; Michael, for example. She lifted her head and watched a white star wink into life just above the northern headland, and hang trembling in the darkening sky.

Star white, star bright…

The childish wishing game she'd played with her mother echoed through her mind. Of course she could be fooling herself, indulging in wishful thinking, hoping of the impossible. And not even to herself did she put into words what that impossible hope might be.

He said in a voice pitched so low she felt it reverberate through his strong chest rather than heard it, 'Are you tired?'

The anticipation that had been building caught fire, persuading her into recklessness. 'A little,' she murmured.

Barely moving, he swung her around in a slow, tight circle. The lean hand on her back slid lower, holding her hips against him. Feverish exaltation soared like sparks through her blood. She tilted her head, looking up into a dark, lean face. Starshine revealed narrowed eyes, a keen predatory look that should have terrified her instead of sending fiery little thrills along every nerve.

Then he smiled, and the heat inside her flared into a divine rashness. 'Perhaps we should go to bed,' he said.

She couldn't speak, but she managed to nod. Yet he didn't carry her off; instead, they danced on like lovers in a dream as his arms came around her, and his head lowered until their lips touched and their feet stilled.

His kiss was a seduction in itself, his mouth sure and gentle, so skilful that a flash of anger lit up her mind. She didn't want this practised, adept love-making; she wanted the half-angry kisses he'd given her before, because he'd barely been able to control them…

Yet she couldn't deny him. Heart to heart, bodies responding to the most elemental communication of all, they kissed until the perfume and sound of the sea permeated her emotions. His kisses lulled her with a honeyed enticement that masked her anger and wooed her into passionate response, so that when he picked her up and carried her into his bedroom she was ready for him, her whole body singing with arousal.

She didn't even look around the room, although she noticed that someone had lit candles there. Their warm, erratic light flickered across Caelan's face, dark, almost stern, its arrogant framework intensely pronounced as he set her on her feet beside a huge bed.

He looked down into her face and said, 'You make me drunk with desire.'

The words seemed torn from him, and were followed by kisses that closed each eye, more to the corners of her trembling mouth, one to the softly throbbing hollow in her throat. Her body became a stranger to her, drugged into heady passion, aching with a craving she'd never experienced before.

She felt his teeth close on an earlobe and shivered at the dart of desire that pierced her. 'You do the same to me,' she said in a voice she didn't recognise.

Delicious shudders of sensation arrowed through her, and she could only stare at him as he shrugged himself out of his coat and shirt.

Her mouth dried. He was magnificent, sleek and olive-tawny in the welcoming light of the candles, his powerful muscles hinting at his great strength as he said, 'Hold up your arms.'

Obediently she did so, and the camisole flowed over her in a susurration of amber silk, leaving her standing in the lace bra and briefs, bought, she realised on a sudden flash of insight, for just this moment.

Caelan's ice-cool eyes flamed the blue of the strongest

heat, and she had to quell an impulse to take an involuntary step back.

'You've always reminded me of some mythical, dangerous creature from a perilous land of faerie,' he said huskily. 'So beautiful, lovely enough to steal a man's courage and wit and sense from him until all he can think of is losing himself in you.'

She was shaking her head, her mouth soft and intensely vulnerable, her green-gold eyes filled with caution. '*La Belle Dame Sans Merci*?' she said, trying so hard to be sophisticated she sounded hard. 'I keep telling you, I'm just an ordinary woman, Caelan.'

His flash of white teeth revealed a smile that was humourless. 'Then why do my hands tremble when I touch you? Look!'

Fascinated, she watched as he stroked up one arm and the long line of her throat, closing her eyes when the delicate torture became unbearable. Her breath came sharply through her lips, and she couldn't bear this intense, tantalising temptation any more.

Yet she had to. Without thinking she mimicked him, smoothing over his sleek hide, her skin tingling at the slight roughness of the pattern of hair as her fingertips explored him. His heat blasted into her, and when he undid the scrap of material around her breasts she felt the rapid thud of his heart against her palms.

It gave her courage enough to let her hands slide down to the top of his trousers, courage enough to lay her cheek against his bare chest, the sound of his heart in her ear, and say, 'You've got too many clothes on.'

He laughed deeply. 'So what do you suggest we do about it?'

Turning her head slightly, she let her lips touch him.

She smiled, a small, secret smile that lingered when he lifted her face to his.

He said harshly, 'So much for any chance of a gentle wooing.'

His mouth closed on hers, and Abby gave herself exultantly, aware that there would be no turning back.

CHAPTER EIGHT

AFTER Abby had wrestled for several seconds with the fastenings of his trousers, Caelan laughed and covered her hands with his. 'I'll do it,' he said.

Was that a note of satisfaction in his voice?

But he didn't immediately strip. Instead he lifted his other hand into her hair, pulling out the clips that held it in place.

'Amber silk,' he murmured, sifting the brilliant sweep of it through his long fingers. 'Like a handful of flames, hot and glowing.' Laughter was a rough purr in the back of his throat and his eyes had glittered like ice-blue diamonds beneath thick black lashes. 'My own personal heat source...'

She thrilled to the raw note in his deep voice, the possessive caress of his hand as he cupped her breasts before bending to kiss each pleading centre, heating her eager body with the blatant aphrodisiac of his touch.

Although she struggled against it, she couldn't suppress a delicious shiver at the erotic contrast of his sleek, tanned body against her paler, more delicate skin. As for the hot, sensory pull of his ardent, skilful mouth and the light of passion that had burned in his eyes...

Then he lifted his head and started to undress.

Skin flushed and eyes dazed, Abby turned a little away, noting the wide, low bed, half covered in mosquito netting. The light coverings had been pushed back.

A moment of sanity made her wonder what on earth she was doing here. Making love with Caelan—with her husband, she thought with a primal frisson—would put her in such danger that she should call a halt right now.

Only she didn't want to.

She gasped when he nipped gently at the exquisitely tender place where her neck met her shoulder.

'Like that?' he murmured, and did it on the other side, sending tormenting rills of pleasure through her as her skin tightened.

'Too much,' she whispered, but he heard her.

'Good.' Again that raw, possessive note edged his tone. He picked her up and came down onto the bed with her, his big body fully aroused, gleaming and bronze and overwhelming.

Abby had little experience to base any expectations on, but she knew what she wanted—to pleasure him as much as he was pleasuring her, and she could only hope that desire would somehow compensate for the expertise he so clearly had in this most intimate of activities.

So, cocooned in his warmth, she touched his chest in shy exploration, her heart rejoicing when that familiar thunder of his heart deepened. Willingly, eagerly, she followed his lead, and lost her own way, falling deeper and deeper into a dark wonderland of the senses until all that mattered was his mouth on her breast, the fire that burned deep in the pit of her belly, and the sensuous glide of skin on skin, the heat of his touch and the glitter in his eyes, and her body's erotic awakening to his expert tuition.

She had no idea she could feel like this—every nerve alert and expectant, so highly strung that pleasure was poised precariously on the cusp between rapture and pain.

In the end she clenched her hands onto his sweat-damp shoulders and gasped incoherently, 'I can't—I don't—Caelan, please.'

He looked at her with smouldering eyes in a drawn, fiercely determined face. 'Yes,' he said thickly. 'It's time.'

Automatically she closed her eyes as he moved over her, then forced them open. This was the first time, and she'd make sure she remembered every second of it.

Candlelight gleamed in a warm patina across shoulders that shut out the rest of the room. Caelan slid his arms beneath her, lifting her slightly, and his mouth drifted down her breast. Fire scorched through her as she felt the full power and weight of his body. She had never, she thought wildly, not even in the hurricane that killed Gemma, felt so out of control, so helpless as she did now.

The erotic tug of his lips on the rosy centre of her breast banished the sad memories. Unable to stop herself, she arched up against him, and he laughed and lifted his head and slowly, steadily, eased his way into her, his eyes holding hers in a stare that held so many levels of meaning she couldn't separate them.

He filled her, and still he pressed on, and miraculously there was room, and with that overwhelming invasion came extreme pleasure, hot and heady and desperate.

Deep inside her a set of muscles she hadn't known she had clamped, holding tight to his long length. He said abruptly, 'Relax.'

'I can't,' she breathed, shocked and startled by her body's takeover of her will and mind.

He smiled, a swift feral movement of his beautiful mouth, and thrust home. Abby cried out, then soared, rocketed, raced into ecstasy, her whole body convulsing around him as sensations joined to send her to another universe where nothing but feeling existed, a transport of ecstasy so intense she thought she might die of it.

Slowly, so slowly she didn't know when it happened,

the delicious rapture faded into an equally delicious languor. But she fought it, finally opening her eyes.

Caelan was lying beside her, his expression so controlled he looked like a bronze mask against the creamy pillows. To her humiliation she couldn't remember him moving, but she knew one thing.

'You didn't,' she began, then closed her eyes in shame. What could she say? *What happened? What are we going to do now?*

'No, I didn't,' he said evenly, a slight note of humour in his voice. 'It's not important.'

'I thought—' She clamped her lips over the incautious words. Embarrassment made her cringe; she was, she thought miserably, the equivalent of those men who took their own satisfaction, then rolled over and went to sleep.

'Don't think,' he said coolly, echoing her thoughts. 'Go to sleep now.'

But she couldn't. Slowly, afraid of a rebuff, she turned into his arms, and kissed his shoulder, letting her lips linger on his skin. He tasted of salt and smoke and a faint musk that fanned her internal fires from a smoulder to an inferno, replacing physical satiation with eager anticipation.

His arms tightened around her and she felt every muscle in his strong body harden. Emboldened, she followed her own inclinations and licked the satiny skin against her lips, savouring the tastes and texture of his skin with unfeigned pleasure.

Shuddering, he said in a rough voice, 'You must be sore.'

She gave an experimental wriggle. 'I've never felt better,' she told him honestly.

He laughed and tilted her face, examining it with merciless, gleaming eyes that set her spine tingling. 'Sure?'

She stretched languorously, sliding against him in a shameless, openly seductive overture. 'Positive,' she said in a tone so demure it sounded smug.

'Then let's try again.'

This time it was slow and tantalising; he took her into realms of physical pleasure she'd never dreamed of until she sobbed for release, her body a taut, desperate bow against his hard, demanding one. This time, when at last she reached the heights they travelled together, tossed by the widening waves of sensation onto some unknown shore of satiation.

Locked in his arms, she fell headlong into sleep.

Michael's voice woke Abby with a start. She sat bolt upright in bed, only to slide hurriedly back under the covers when she realised she was naked. Caelan was gone; she heard his voice too, and realised that, far from standing in the doorway, Michael was some distance away, and that Caelan was with him.

On the beach, probably.

Colour burned up through her skin as she slid out of bed. At least she'd have clothes on when she met Caelan's ironic gaze. She picked up her pretty silk suit and the bra and briefs and scurried down the short hallway to the room she'd dressed in before that short, poignant wedding.

A long shower later, she walked into the wardrobe and examined the clothes there, still unable to believe that they were all hers.

Shopping with Caelan had been an odd experience. They'd stopped outside an empty salon, and she'd said, 'It looks as though they've closed.'

'For us,' he said with a shrug of his magnificent shoulders.

Sure enough, the door opened as soon as he'd rung the bell, and the owner, a very chic woman in her mid-forties, smiled at Caelan. She closed the door and with a murmured 'This way, Mr Bagaton,' escorted them into a private room with a fitting room at the other end.

Completely at home in such exotic surroundings, Caelan said, 'My fiancée wants clothes—casual ones for the summer.'

The owner nodded, surveying Abby with a measuring gaze that made her feel as though she were stripped of clothes. 'We have a new designer who should suit very well.'

Striving not to sound rude and abrupt, Abby produced a stiff smile for him. 'You might as well go—I'm sure you'll find this horribly boring.'

His smile was intimate and incredibly heady; only she could see the glint of mockery in his crystalline eyes. 'At the moment I can think of nothing more interesting than watching you parade for me.'

Abby heard a stifled sigh from the woman behind, but pride kept her head high and her face rigid. He was determined to make sure she bought what he considered a suitable wardrobe.

'I've never paraded before, but I'll do my best,' she said.

Driven by recklessness and that disturbing sense of being herded into a trap, she came out of the fitting room like a model on show, breasts jutting, hips swaying, flicking her hair carelessly when she turned after letting her eyes drift over Caelan in a parody of catwalk aloofness.

He lifted an ironic eyebrow, but the blue gleam in his gaze scared her into a return to common sense. The raw attraction between them was dangerous enough without her stoking it.

Surprisingly he and she had the same taste in clothes. And he had a good eye for the perfect accessory.

But then, she thought trenchantly, no doubt he'd had a lot of experience in buying clothes for his various lovers.

Had he really been celibate since they'd met all those years ago? It didn't seem possible—and it wasn't sensible to think about it.

Together, with minimal input from her, he and the forbiddingly discreet salon owner chose a wardrobe to see her through her sojourn in Dacia. Common sense muted any protest; Caelan knew what would be acceptable, and the salon owner certainly knew how to achieve results that transformed her client from an ordinary New Zealand woman to the faintly mysterious, exotic wife of a princely tycoon.

'Cosmetics,' Caelan said, getting to his feet. A faint smile crossed his face as he glanced at his watch before surveying Abby's face. 'Do you know what you want?'

'Yes, of course.'

He inclined his dark head. 'Then I'll pick you up in an hour.' He looked at the salon owner. 'You'll deliver?'

'Of course,' she said instantly, dropping a pen in her haste to take down the address of the apartment.

Of course, Abby thought cynically. With the lure of future sales, all things were possible. Caelan smiled and thanked her, and both women watched his tall, lean body move with a prowling, lethal grace out of the room.

The older woman was the first to pull herself together, but a certain glow in her eyes revealed that the full impact of Caelan's potent masculinity wasn't lost on her. Flushing slightly, she said, 'I believe there is a wedding suit to choose. I have found what I think is the perfect one for you, but of course the decision must be yours.'

But there had been no decision to make; Abby had fallen in love with it at first sight.

And then the salon owner had said, 'Forgive me for saying this, but you need underclothes to wear those clothes as they should be worn. I'll get a fitter to bring in a selection for you.'

By now Abby had no pride left. 'Thank you.'

'And what brand of cosmetics do you prefer?'

The cheapest brand of generic moisturiser in the supermarket, Abby thought cynically, but she picked a name at random.

'An excellent line.'

Determined not to splash out, Abby stuck to basic underwear, although she allowed herself the sybaritic luxury of several silk camisoles and matching briefs. And when it came to cosmetics, the consultant persuaded her to indulge not only in a basic skin-care regime, but also a slick, gold-tinged lipstick and a seductive, subtle eyeshadow that turned her eyes to smoky green jewels.

Now, with the flight to Dacia only eight hours away, she was glad she'd let herself be talked into spending so much of Caelan's money. She needed, she thought mordantly, all the help she could get.

So she chose a sundress in smoky shades of green and gold, only to stare at her shoulders in shock. Theirs had been a long, sinfully gentle loving, but, even with Caelan tempering his great strength to her slender body, he had left faint marks on her. Hastily scrambling into a pair of trousers and a short-sleeved cotton shirt, she remembered biting his shoulder in a moment of ecstasy and thought with an odd twist of sensation that she'd branded him too.

For better or for worse, they were married. This, she thought as she closed the door behind herself, is going to be as good as it gets. The sex was a bonus; for her it had been frighteningly wonderful, but perhaps for Caelan it was simply more of the same.

It wasn't true happiness, but it had to be enough. Deliberately relaxing her facial muscles, she went out into the first day of her marriage.

It turned out to be so busy that after the first few moments she didn't have time to dwell on the future. Shortly before lunch they left in the helicopter for Auckland, and that afternoon all three Bagatons met the caseworker assigned to the adoption process.

Later in the day, when the private jet had reached cruising height, Abby said, 'What did you think of her?'

'Damned difficult to fool,' Caelan returned. 'And determined to make sure that Michael's rights are safeguarded.'

But for all her professionalism, the woman hadn't been immune to Caelan's cool masculinity. Was anyone? Abby wondered, smiling down at Michael's excited face. No woman, anyway. The caseworker noted that Michael seemed perfectly happy with both parents, but presumably she'd been looking for signs that would warn her all wasn't as it seemed in their picture-perfect family.

She yawned, a brief memory of making love to Caelan lighting treacherous embers in the pit of her stomach. Her body ached with a feverish languor that sapped her energy and summoned more vivid images of them together.

She quelled it firmly. Ahead of them lay a long flight. Although she'd made sure that the plane had everything necessary to keep Michael happy, she didn't fool herself that it would be easy.

In the end though, the journey went with remarkable ease. Keeping a lid on Michael's high spirits hadn't been nearly so difficult with Caelan as back-up. Abby looked down at Dacia, an emerald in an enamelled blue sea, and wondered whether she was dreaming. Only a week ago she'd been tense and edgy, bent on escaping from Nukuroa to a safer haven, yet aware that her life would be spent looking over her shoulder. And worrying whether by fulfilling Gemma's wishes she was depriving Michael of much that was important to him.

Now, half a world away, ears popping as the jet eased itself towards the runway, she was astonished at how much had changed in those short days.

A movement beside her brought her out of her reverie. 'Abby, my ears hurt,' Michael wailed.

'Swallow hard,' she told him. 'Have you finished your toffee? You could give a big yawn and see if that makes your ear feel better.'

After a prodigious gape, he screwed up his face and said earnestly, 'I think another toffee would make it better.'

From the corner of her eye Abby caught a flash of white as Caelan smiled. Her heart jumped in her chest.

No, she wasn't going to think of how her attitude had changed since he'd walked into her hall at Nukuroa.

Instead, she'd remember how unfailingly helpful he'd been during the long, often tedious flight. It warmed her heart to see the slow blossoming of his relationship with Michael.

He might not know much about children, but his tactics were working; Michael loved being treated as an equal. Once she'd looked up from her book to see them playing chess, both absorbed and intent as Caelan showed his nephew the moves.

She watched carefully, relaxing when she realised that Michael was thoroughly enjoying himself. Later, when he was asleep, she said, 'Thank you for entertaining him. I'd never have thought of playing chess with him.'

'It's a war game,' he said laconically, 'and most young boys enjoy it. My father taught me. Do you play?'

'Yes,' she said. 'My mother adored it, and she was a killer. I used to call her Attila the Hun.'

He looked a little startled at that. On a gleam of amusement she said, 'Enjoyment of tactical games isn't confined to the male sex, you know.'

'I'd like to have met your mother.'

But he didn't look convinced and Abby wondered whether he thought such pursuits were unfeminine.

She said, 'Tell me something about your family in Dacia. I mean, I know of your cousin the prince, because his wife is a New Zealander and their wedding got huge publicity at home. And of course I know Princess Lucia a little. But there's another cousin, Prince Guy—the computer man, who turns up in newspapers now and then.'

'He's married to Lauren, a charming Englishwoman.'

She said wistfully, 'I envy you these cousins. As far as I know, I don't have any relatives.'

'The word in Dacian has a much wider meaning than in English. We are all descended from a ruling prince— not the same one.'

Curiously she asked, 'So how did a Dacian prince end up a New Zealand citizen?'

'I have dual citizenship. My father came out to New Zealand and I grew up there.' He'd emigrated because his second much-younger wife had developed a crush on another man; instead of seeing her emotional unfaithfulness as an indication of her character, Caelan thought cynically, his father had blamed her lover.

And the move hadn't worked. His stepmother had hated New Zealand, calling it a provincial little country on the edge of nowhere. But he'd learned to love it, and his dual nationality was a natural expression of his feelings.

He leaned back in the seat and surveyed her with narrowed eyes. 'You're scared.'

'Nervous,' she corrected smartly.

And still not convinced she'd done the right thing. There was a distance about her that piqued his hunter's instincts.

'Stop worrying. You liked Cia and Hunt, didn't you?'

'Yes,' she admitted.

'Then you'll like the rest of my family; they're just like any other.'

Three weeks later she understood what he meant. And how utterly wrong he'd been. Although the welcome from the prince and princess had warmed and comforted her, no other family she knew called a huge pile of honey-coloured stone the Little Palace, because the other one on the island, the Old Palace, was twice its size and built on the foundations of a Roman fortress.

No New Zealand family wore priceless jewels with such insouciance, or partied in immense salons lined with panelling and mirrors, fragrant with exquisite flowers and lit by candelabra in a timeless, romantic atmosphere of tradition and privilege.

No other New Zealand family drove to the accompaniment of smiles and toots and waves from every other road user. And none was related to every European royal family, those still in their thrones and those adjusting to lives as exiles.

She had been eased skilfully into Dacian social life, shocked when she realised that her name was appearing more and more in the Court Circular sent to the media by the royal household.

Caelan had kept his word. At every public function he was beside her, guiding her safely through parties and sailing trips, family picnics and the annual garden party, a glittering opera première for charity, the opening of an art exhibition in the Old Palace down by the harbour, dinners and receptions that ranged from formal to pleasantly casual.

Yet not the Caelan she'd known in New Zealand. Like her, he was playing a part, and perhaps only she could tell that whatever closeness had been forged by their wedding night had gone. He wasn't even staying in the palace; apparently he owned a house on the southern coast, and that was where he was living.

Tonight was their engagement ball; the official photographs taken the day after their arrival had been released with the announcement of their engagement that afternoon. Bells had rung across Dacia the moment the news was out, and fireworks were already flowering in the soft Mediterranean dusk.

Tomorrow there would be an interview with the only two journalists that Caelan had decided would be allowed near them.

And now, clad in a sensuous dress the exact green of her eyes, she watched the maid pin back her hair with five emerald stars while her stomach clamped tight in apprehension, because the extended family had arrived, and tonight she was officially on show. Her engagement ring, a glorious emerald flanked by two diamonds, glittered like another star on her hand.

Someone knocked on the door and the maid made an excuse and left the room.

Frozen with nervousness, Abby took several deep, grounding breaths, but when she recognised Alexa's voice she relaxed a little. Her hostess, Prince Luka's wife, was a lovely person; she'd been a staunch support, help-ing Abby tactfully through the intricacies of protocol and family dynamics.

The maid appeared in the door. 'Ma'am, the princess would like to see you.'

Abby got to her feet and dragged in another breath. 'Of course,' she said, and walked out into the bedroom.

The princess was radiant in satin, its tawny hue a con-trast to the magnificent Dacian emeralds in her necklace and tiara.

'Oh, Abby,' she said, and came towards her with a smile. 'You look glorious! Maria's done a brilliant job with your hair.' The maid bobbed a little curtsey and withdrew. 'And your emeralds pick up the green in your eyes. How are you feeling?'

'Terrified.' Abby didn't mind telling her; although Alexa's grandfather had been the ruling prince of Illyria, another Mediterranean princedom, his love affair with her grandmother had finished before he'd known of her preg-nancy, so Alexa had grown up in New Zealand with no idea of her heritage. Abby clung to the knowledge that if the princess could adjust to this whole splendid, glam-orous ambience, so could she.

Except that the princess knew she was loved; although she and her husband didn't flaunt their feelings they ran deep and true, a powerful current between them that glo-rified their lives. For the first time in her life Abby un-derstood envy.

The princess laughed. 'I know, believe me, the family *en masse* can look intimidating, but they're lovely people. Well, most of them.'

'How on earth can you fill a ballroom with relatives? Somehow I got the idea from Caelan that there weren't all that many.'

'Ah, he conveniently forgot to mention that even if the link is five hundred years back the family connection is kept.'

'He did indeed,' Abby said colourlessly.

Apart from a few rare moments, she hadn't been alone with Caelan since they'd arrived. When they weren't socialising he and Prince Luka had been secluded in various meetings while she and the rest of the royal family took the first tentative footsteps towards friendship.

Michael had been a great help there. The palace nursery was noisy with children—the two hearty boys who lived there and Princess Lucia's charming, strong-minded little daughter had welcomed Michael with enthusiasm and interest. All asleep now, tucked up after a glorious afternoon spent at a secluded bay surrounded by pine and olive trees.

Abby confessed, 'I'm scared of making Caelan look an idiot by forgetting who's who, or mispronouncing their names.'

'You couldn't make Caelan look an idiot however hard you tried,' Alexa said affectionately. 'He's idiot-proof. All the Bagaton men are. And remember, the family is quite accustomed to the Bagatons choosing the people they love and marry! Luka's poor parents were the last to be forced into a dynastic marriage, and he vowed that neither he nor anyone else in his family would have to do that.'

But that was exactly what Caelan was facing—a marriage of convenience established to safeguard his sister's son.

Perhaps the princess had caught a flash of Abby's misery. She said comfortingly, 'Caelan will look after you. If you don't already know it, he's an intensely protective man.' She gave a quick, far from regal, grin. 'And a possessive one—it's rather fun for all of us to see how carefully he watches over you! Now, come. And enjoy yourself tonight!'

CHAPTER NINE

THE last thing Abby expected from her own engagement ball was enjoyment, but it happened, mostly, she realised with an odd pang of fear, because Caelan was always there, supportive and reassuring and intensely compelling.

So during the first waltz, with everyone crowded around and clapping, she let herself relax against his lean, hard strength and gave herself over to the music, a Viennese tune she'd never thought to dance to with the man she resented and wanted in equal measure.

He murmured, 'I hear our son swam a whole ten metres by himself this afternoon.'

Startled, she looked up, and he smiled. Heart thumping, she said, 'He did, and you should have seen his face when he realised he'd done it! You've never referred to him as your son before.'

'From now on he's *our* son. I agree that he should know who his birth parents are, but he's lucky enough to have two sets.' And before she could reply to that, he went on, 'You look radiant. Every inch a princess.'

Somehow the raw edge to his voice gave life to his practised compliment; when he spoke like that, she foolishly wanted to believe that none of it was deliberate, that he really meant each word.

'I—thank you. So do you,' she returned automatically, then flushed. 'Look like a prince, I mean. Champagne must have addled my brain.'

'One glass—and barely touched at that—shouldn't do that,' he responded on a dry, amused note.

Somehow she had to come to some accommodation with her unruly emotions, she thought desperately. They could do this, make a happy family for the child she loved; she mustn't let her feelings stand in the way of Michael's security. That was the whole reason for this glittering, elaborate farce.

Caelan was declaring to his family and the world that he valued her enough to make her his wife. The fact that it was based on a lie—that if it hadn't been for Michael there would have been no wedding, no future, no happy family—was their secret.

But she'd noticed a difference in him the moment they'd set foot on Dacia. Outwardly he'd been everything a woman would want in a lover—but instead of the forthright, formidable man she'd dealt with honestly in New Zealand, he'd retreated behind an impenetrable façade. In a week's time they'd be married according to Dacia's laws. They'd spend four days alone in a villa on the south coast of Dacia, then fly back to New Zealand.

And then what?

A life where superb sex and money replaced any communion of spirit and mind? A fierce pang of longing, of despair, ached through her. Defiantly she banished it. All right, so she'd always hoped for a marriage like her parents', but she was the one who'd made it impossible; her actions had brought Caelan to hunt her down like some dark nemesis.

And even knowing what she did now, she still couldn't work out whether she'd change a thing.

'Smile,' Caelan commanded, the word flicking her like a whip.

She looked up into a dark, absorbed face, into eyes that gleamed with hard mockery.

'Smile,' he said again, and lifted her hand to his mouth.

An anguished pleasure shot through her, setting her blood coursing, her thoughts tumbling endlessly. She was saved from melting by the glint of satisfaction in his gaze; he knew that he had only to touch her to let loose that bewildering passion.

Caelan wondered exactly what was going on in the brain behind those great, tilted eyes, shielded from his scrutiny by the heavy curtain of her lashes. Then, as he kissed her hand, defiance smouldered in their depths and she curved her hand against his mouth before moving it to his cheek, letting her fingertips linger as though she couldn't bear to break the contact.

Her smile, mysterious and a little taunting, made promises.

Every muscle in his body tightened. Without exception his mistresses had been experienced women, skilled in the arts of love, but none of them had been able to stir his blood like Abby.

'Why?' she breathed, and smiled, a slow, heady movement of her lush mouth.

Not only did she look like some mysterious woman out of myth, but she possessed a subtle sexuality that drew him as inexorably as though she'd put a spell on him.

He despised himself for that lack of self-control, so his voice was harsh when he said, 'We're meant to be in love.'

Abby barely heard the words, but her body sprang to life at the rough note of hunger in it.

The rest of the evening passed like a dream, a whirl

of good wishes and laughter and music, of colour and glitter and the perfume of flowers. And of Caelan, always there, coolly protective, letting that controlled sexual response stand in for the love everyone took for granted.

In the small hours of the morning they drove back through the scented night to the palace, where he kissed her hand in a formal salute and left. Exhausted, she went up to her bedroom. The maid stood up as she came in.

Summoning a smile, Abby said, 'I thought I told you not to wait up.'

The middle-aged woman said serenely, 'We Dacians are independent. We do what we want to, and I want to help you. Prince Caelan is much loved here, and it is a privilege to tend to his bride.'

They were all so kind, while she and Caelan were lying to them. Did the end ever justify the means? It had to— Michael's welfare was more important than any private emotions she and Caelan had to endure.

Abby crawled into bed, only to lie awake for hours. Her resolution never to let herself soften towards him was being sorely tested. Oh, she could cope with the fierce, wildfire passion that flared between them, but this reluctant appreciation was dangerous. It mined away at her independence. She'd been safer, her integrity less in jeopardy, when they'd been at daggers drawn.

'It's a matter of policy for him,' she said out loud, listening to the quiet sounds of a Mediterranean night.

As well as convincing the world—and the New Zealand social welfare system—that they were in love, Caelan would appreciate that a complaisant wife was much easier to live with than one who held aloof.

And her defiant attitude had been a mistake; his whole career proclaimed that he enjoyed a challenge. It would give him cynical satisfaction to turn her lovesick like his other mistresses.

So she wouldn't let it happen.

Eventually sleep claimed her, but only to inflict dreams on her, in which she ran endlessly from some hideous, terrifying being, only to force herself to turn and see that it was Caelan.

And she didn't have to search far to find a meaning to that! Once again she was being forced in a direction she didn't want to go, and the resentment she'd used to defend herself seemed a weak, futile emotion. Telling herself that his charm and wit and thoughtfulness were all false didn't help; each day that passed she felt the ground beneath her feet become more and more shaky.

Over the next week the tempo picked up. The wedding was to be held in a chapel at the Old Palace—'To give the people a chance to see you both,' Alexa said cheerfully. 'Dacians adore weddings.' She gave Abby a glance. 'All well?'

'Fine, thank you,' Abby said automatically, and summoned a smile. On an impulse she asked, 'How do you cope? You were brought up like me—ordinary. And so was Lauren, and Princess Ianthe of Illyria—another New Zealander. How on earth do you all deal with living in the public eye?'

They had retired to Alexa's private sitting room after a reception for local dignitaries. Alexa put her teacup and saucer down and said thoughtfully, 'Ianthe and I fell in love with men who made it perfectly clear that they came with a country attached. We had to choose whether or not to accept that.'

Ah, there was the source of her anguish in a nutshell. They had had a choice; Abby had none. But in spite of the questioning note in the princess's final sentence she couldn't admit that to this charming, warm woman.

Infusing her voice with a confidence she was far from feeling, she said, 'I'll get used to it. And at home it's not so—so different. We lead a much less structured life there.'

'From what Caelan said, you'll be travelling with him, at least until Michael goes to school. And there will always be formal occasions—which you seem to enjoy. You certainly don't show any sign of nerves.'

'Because Caelan's always there,' Abby said on a wry note.

'Of course he is. He wants you to be happy.' Alexa leaned forward. 'I think you're worrying unnecessarily. You have lovely manners, and it's only a matter of time before you become completely confident.'

'Actually,' Abby confided, 'everyone's been so nice that I'm not paranoid about that now. What really worries me is the thought of the media.'

The princess nodded, her face bleak. 'The wretched paparazzi! Only a couple of weeks ago Luka had one thrown off the island—he'd taken photos of our children.'

With a shiver, Abby muttered, 'I wish Caelan were just an ordinary man.'

'No, you don't,' Alexa said firmly. 'If you'd wanted an ordinary man you'd have fallen in love with one! As for the hounds of the press—yes, they're a nuisance and so is the constant attention, but love makes it all worthwhile.'

Uncomfortably Abby nodded. 'Yes,' she said simply, knowing that this was true, 'love makes anything worthwhile.'

But she wouldn't let herself love Caelan. She didn't dare.

The princess held her eyes for a few tense seconds, then gave a smile. 'Cling to that,' she advised. 'It does help. And remember that you're a New Zealander—infinitely adaptable!'

Abby kept those last words in her mind during the tumultuous week before the wedding, holding them close like a mantra as she walked up the aisle towards Caelan, magnificent in formal, superbly cut clothes, Prince Luka beside him.

For this wedding she wore a classically cut dress in cream silk that had been made by a Dacian couturier with magic in her fingers. The emerald stars held her veil in place above hair plaited in a formal French pleat at the nape of her neck. Behind her walked Michael and the royal children, the boys solemn in page-boys' satins, the two little Illyrian princesses in soft, summery clothes with flowers in their hair.

Hunt Radcliffe gave her away. Halfway up the aisle he murmured, 'How many nannies have you got posted around this chapel?'

'One for each child,' she whispered as the triumphal chorus swelled about her.

He said, 'With whips, I hope.'

So she was smiling when she reached the man who waited for her in front of the altar, his blue eyes hooded and gleaming beneath black lashes, his handsome face a bronze mask in the light of the candles.

Afterwards Abby couldn't remember much about the service beyond Caelan's deep tone as he made his vows, and the whisper and sigh of silk and satin as the congregation rose to greet them when they came back down the aisle.

Then the bells rang out across the city, mingling with the cheers of the Dacian crowds, and in the open carriage behind flower-decked white horses Caelan's hand closed around hers, warm and strong and firm as they drove back to the reception.

That and the wedding feast passed in a blur too, but at last it was over and she was kissing Michael goodbye, saying, 'We'll be back in four more sleeps, darling. Be good while we're gone, won't you, and have fun in the pool.'

He beamed at her. 'Uncle Caelan says I can go out on the boat with him when we get home.'

'That will be lovely.' She gave him a quick, hard hug and straightened. This was the first time they'd been separated, and she hated leaving him.

'But only if you keep practising that swimming,' Caelan said. He stooped and picked Michael up. 'Be good,' he said, and kissed his cheek.

Michael hugged him fiercely, clinging when Caelan went to put him down. He said in an unhappy little voice, 'I want to come with you.'

Abby hesitated, but before she had time to answer, Caelan said, 'You told your cousins you'd stay with them. A promise is a promise, Michael.'

His face crumpled, but he swallowed manfully, eyes wide and gathering tears.

'We won't be away long,' Abby said, heart contracting.

Caelan relinquished him into the care of his special nursemaid and said, 'We'll bring you a present when we come back.'

He nodded and Caelan took Abby's arm and steered her away, saying pleasantly, 'Don't look so tragic. People will wonder if we've had our first quarrel.'

'Little do they know,' she said, but her voice wobbled.

'He'll be fine. Would you like to bring his nursemaid back to New Zealand with us?'

She stared at him. 'Why a Dacian?'

He shrugged. 'Because he likes her. And so that she could teach him Dacian and Italian. I've checked Ilana's credentials—she's been trained in an excellent school, and, yes, she'd like to travel.'

Official goodbyes all said, they were on the way to the helicopter pad. Abby felt a chill at the thought of another woman in Michael's life, then chided herself. It was stupid to be jealous; soon he'd be going to school, and the words 'my teacher says' would ring in her ears with all the authority of holy writ!

As for the deeper, more shameful fear—Caelan had married her; he wouldn't be scheming to replace her with a nanny so that he could divorce her! A glance at his face wasn't exactly reassuring. Hard and forceful, it was the face of a man who, as Lucia had said, knew what he wanted and was utterly sure that he'd get it.

What have I done? she thought, on a swift kick of panic. This complex, tough, clever man is my husband!

She said, 'It's important for him to speak Dacian, isn't it?'

Caelan glanced at her. 'It's a common bond in the family,' he said after a moment. 'I'd like my children to be fluent in it.'

'Your *children*?' It emerged in an astounded squeak, but inside her some renegade emotion melted a hard knot of resentment.

Caelan's brows lifted. '*Our* children,' he amended smoothly.

And then they were ambushed by a laughing crowd of wedding guests, and escorted to the chopper pad amid a hail of sugar almonds and flowers. Once in the helicopter Abby picked rose petals off her skirt and thought of Caelan's smooth assumption that they'd be having other children.

Over the past weeks on Dacia she'd managed to push the memory of her wedding night in New Zealand to the back of her mind. Except late at night, she conceded. And in her dreams…

But clearly he meant it to be a full marriage in every way.

Well, why not? the cynical part of her mind asked unanswerably. He was a virile man with a great appetite for sex, and he'd promised faithfulness. Naturally he'd want to make love to the woman he'd forced into marriage.

And she, she knew with a painful twist of the heart, would enjoy it with rapture tinctured with bitterness. She recalled various women at the wedding—titled, elegant, exquisite, who navigated their way through society with a skill that came from being born to it. She'd noticed an occasional glance at her, slightly bewildered, even pitying; they still made her cringe.

Caelan could have married any one of the flock of princezas, marquesas, countesses and gräfins who'd decorated the occasion so suitably.

Yes, Alexa and Ianthe had made lives for themselves in this exclusive social milieu. But they had talents— Princess Ianthe of Illyria was a brilliant scientist, her work on the fresh-water dolphins of Illyria world-famous. Alexa was a superbly creative photographer. Of the other wives in the Dacian royal family, Princess Lucia was a Bagaton by birth, and Lauren, the exquisite Englishwoman married to Prince Guy, had carved her way through the financial world and now ran a charity

she'd set up to help children in the third world achieve
education.

And, that coolly logical part of her prompted, they love
their husbands and they know their husbands love them.

It was simple as that. She'd always be the interloper
with no glittering talent to offer, unloved and unloving;
the best she could hope for was to settle into some sort
of affection as the years went by and she became the
mother of Caelan's children.

A wave of intense dejection shocked her. Summoning
pride to her aid, she fought it grimly. At least this way
she kept her self-respect. How humiliating it would be to
have been like his previous mistresses and let herself fall
in love with him, yearning pitiably for his love in return!

She wouldn't let it happen. But neither self-respect nor
pride banished the lingering aftermath of pain.

Shocking her with its unexpectedness, strong tanned
fingers closed over hers. Caelan leaned towards her and
said, 'He'll be all right. He's having the time of his life
with the other children, and Alexa has promised to tuck
him up each night.'

She nodded, not daring to look at him in case he realised that she hadn't been worrying about Michael. The
helicopter swooped low over a pine forest, and Caelan
touched her shoulder and pointed. 'The villa. It's close
enough so that if he gets too upset, we can be back in
less than an hour.'

Don't be so thoughtful! she commanded silently, turning her head to stare through the window. His consider-
ation undermined the defences she was struggling to keep
intact.

Perched on a cliff overlooking the Mediterranean, the
honeymoon villa gleamed white in the rapidly fading
daylight. Abby made out a tennis court, a swimming pool

still brilliantly blue, colonnades that would shade the
walls against the midday heat, and enclosed courtyards
where the silver gleam of water hinted at the music of
fountains and rills. The sombre darkness of a pine forest
crowded against an ancient wall on the landward side,
and between them and the sea gardens stretched out,
shadowy and inviting, with splashes of bold colour.

A path led from the landing pad through the pines. As
they walked through the scented shade towards the mansion, Abby drew in a long breath. 'It's beautiful.'

'It began life as a fortress built by one of my more
piratical ancestors to control the seaway,' Caelan told her
drily. 'Whenever a sail was sighted ships would set off
from the harbour and demand a toll, backed up by guns
from the fortress. Everyone made a nice living for a couple of centuries.'

Fascinating facts that only served to underline the huge
difference in their worlds. 'What happened?'

'Oh, things changed,' he said, not hiding the irony in
his voice. 'Robber princes stopped being fashionable, so
the then prince, a very practical man, set his mind to
more respectable ways of earning a living.'

'What about the villagers?'

What did he plan for tonight? Did he expect to take
her to bed? Heated anticipation roiled endlessly inside
her, inextricably mingling with fear and tension.

He grinned. 'Trust you to worry about the villagers.
They turned to fishing and tourism. Less exciting, but just
as profitable in the long term.'

Abby tried to squelch a feverish thrill by reminding
herself that he'd made no attempt to be alone with her
during the past month; every kiss had been formal, every
glance in public had been measured, calculated to con-

vince anyone who watched them that they were truly in love.

Instead of wondering if they'd spend the night together, she should be refusing to consider making love—sex, she corrected herself bleakly. Passionate it might be—would be—but it would also be a soulless coupling, one of convenience; each cynically making use of the other's body for loveless pleasure.

The scent of the pines floated around them, clean and crisp, underlain with that particular fragrance she'd always remember when she thought of Dacia—a soft, fresh commingling of salt and lavender and flowers, sweet, earthy and intensely evocative.

'Welcome to our Dacian home,' Caelan said outside the huge panelled door that looked as though it had survived from the original fortress.

He picked her up, ignoring her shocked exclamation, and strode into the cool, candle-lit interior.

Heart jolting in forbidden expectation, she said unevenly, 'I didn't realise that carrying a bride over the threshold was a tradition in Dacia.'

He stopped and looked down at her, pale eyes glinting in his dark face. 'I make my own traditions,' he drawled, and bent his head and took her startled mouth in a frankly sensual kiss that told her exactly what he planned to do for the rest of the night.

And she, poor fool that she was, craved it just as much as he did.

'I've been wanting to do that for weeks,' he said, letting her slide down his body as he set her on her feet again. He touched her lips with a lean forefinger, the possessive light in his eyes still very pronounced, then said calmly, 'Come out and look at the view. By now there should be enough of a moon to set it off.'

With his scent in her nostrils and her heart jumping nervously, she was ushered through the villa, a magnificent building furnished in what she'd come to label the Dacian style—a skilful, serene combination of antiques and modern pieces, set off with flowers and stunning art. It reminded her of the apartment in Auckland.

He took her out onto a terrace, wide and shaded in part by a pergola covered in vines. Somewhere she could hear a Spanish guitar; it had been her mother's favourite instrument, and difficult tears stung her eyes as the mellow, oddly oriental timbre fell seductively on the night air.

Silently Abby walked across to the edge, and stopped, gasping; the villa seemed to be floating, with nothing but shimmering sea below and a moon as ripe and golden as an orange queening it over the sky.

'I think we should have a glass of champagne.' Caelan walked lithely over to a table where a bottle in a silver ice bucket waited. He poured two glasses, and brought them across to her, handing her one.

'To the future,' he said.

Thinly, her words falling into the quiet air, she repeated the words, and drank with him, taking the opportunity to move a few steps away on the pretext of looking out at the view.

He glanced down at her, his hard face challenging. 'What are you thinking?'

Her face clamped, thoughts and emotions locked behind a proud, sinfully sexy mask as she set the champagne flute onto a side table with a flick of her long, elegant fingers. His skin tightened when he remembered the erotic play of her hands over his body, the way she'd stroked him as though she adored the feel of him and the taste of him in her mouth...

Desire blasted through him like a neutron bomb, so

powerful he had to turn slightly to hide the betrayal of his body.

Abby said remotely, 'That this is an outrageously beautiful place with a fantastic view. How much time do you spend here?'

He swung around to meet her flat, empty gaze.

She was as stubborn as he'd often been accused of being; tough-minded and determined not to give an inch. Somewhere, a rather too-literal fate must be killing itself with mocking laughter, he thought cynically. Several times his conscience had made him break off a relationship because his current lover had fancied herself in love with him. He'd refused to use them like that. Now the woman he'd married flatly refused to do so.

Gemma would have said that it served him right.

His brows rose, but his voice was level, a lazy note of amusement more obvious when he returned, 'I come here as often as I can—usually three to four times a year.' His voice changed. 'Do you know what's really outrageous about this whole situation? It's outrageous that every time I look at you I want you.'

Her breath locked in her throat and her heart contracted into a hard ball in her chest. Torn by longing, she knew that love was the only sensible reason for taking that final step into surrender—and Caelan didn't love her.

He would never love her.

But you don't love him, some treacherous part of her murmured beguilingly, so that makes it fair enough to both of you. No lies, no false hopes.

She winced. 'It's not enough,' she said stonily.

His mouth hardening into a line she recognised, he came towards her. 'It's all we've got, Abby.'

'No,' she blurted, panicked into retreating behind an

elegant wrought-iron chair—a dead give-away to the emotions that were tearing at her.

All her pragmatism about their marriage, their future, was revealed as shoddy rationalisation, based on a cowardly desire for sex without commitment. She had promised herself to this man, to a future together, and that involved sex, so why the virginal flutterings and fears?

Caelan said impatiently, 'No? So you admit it's not all we've got.'

She chose words carefully, infusing each one with sombre conviction. 'I meant no, I refuse to let you bulldoze me into something I'm not ready for.' But one look at his face, cold and brutally determined, warned her she wasn't getting through to him.

'You were ready for it a month ago.'

Her instinct for self-defence, backed by a primitive fear, prompted her next defiant statement. 'I know. But sex is not enough to base a relationship on.'

'Do you want more than sex?' he asked, eyes glinting and keen.

Warning bells clanged. She'd known when she married him that she was taking a huge risk. After all, what did an ordinary woman have in common with a man descended from a line of autocratic princes? A man who'd been born rich, and built himself an even greater empire in the cut-throat world of international finance?

Nothing, she thought bleakly. But for Michael's sake she'd been forced to accept the challenge. Amazingly the resentment that had burned so brightly now flickered.

After a deep breath she said quietly, 'I—I don't know what I want. To be honest, I think.'

'I've been honest,' he said impatiently. 'You've known right from the start that I want you. Are you going to cower behind that chair all night? Grant me a little control; I don't intend to leap on you.'

'I'm tired.' Stung and shaken, she turned away.

She'd taken two steps when his hand on her shoulder froze her. 'Running away isn't going to help. We need to come to a decision.' His voice was cold and authoritative, for all the world as though she were a junior executive who'd admitted a mistake.

Abby swung around to confront him, eyes blazing green. 'When you say *we*, you mean that *you'll* make any decision,' she said, using contempt to cut the moment short. She was too vulnerable, every sense heightened, every nerve quivering. 'You can do that on your own. Let me go.'

The pupils in his pale eyes expanded until they were night-dark, surrounded by a thin circle of ice-blue. Her breath faltered, and she had to swallow to moisten her suddenly dry mouth. Get out of here, the last remnant of common sense warned. *Run!*

Caelan caught her flailing hand and lifted it to his mouth. Holding her startled gaze with his, he kissed the back. The heat of his mouth against her skin sent signals to every pleasure point in her body, curling her fingers in tormented need as she fought the swift expansion of hunger, the tightness in her breasts and their sensitive tips.

'Caelan, this isn't the way—'

Pulses jerking, she tried to wrench free, but he turned her hand over, and this time, instead of a brief brush of his lips against the skin, he bit the mount of Venus under her thumb, his teeth lightly closing on the fine, too-receptive skin.

Lightning stabs of sensation rioted through her, setting her afire. And then he let her go.

'There, that wasn't so bad, was it?' His beautiful mouth curved in cold irony as he stepped back so she could pass him.

Seared by angry chagrin, she stiffened her shoulders and spine and stepped away. 'This is not going to work,' she snapped, 'if you keep mauling me all the time.'

He gave a sudden crack of mirthless laughter. 'You've led a very sheltered life if you thought that that was mauling,' he said cruelly. 'Perhaps I should show you the difference.'

'No!'

But it was too late. Caelan spun her round, deftly and ruthlessly blocking her blows before they reached his solar plexus. His fingers closed around each hand, pushing them behind her back while his head came down and he kissed her with a hard, driving urgency that sliced through her pathetic defences like a sword through satin.

Abby's wild response shocked her into a momentary stillness, just long enough for primeval emotions to shut down her resistance. Her mouth softened and opened under his, the magic of his kiss summoning an untamed heat that melted her into passionate surrender. Desperate, she tried to bring up her knee, only to be foiled by Caelan's strength.

He was aroused—as aroused as she was. And although she was sure he'd planned to teach her a lesson, she felt the abrupt change in him when the kiss transmuted to a potent assault on every sense she owned.

A shameless, risky delight purred through her; she angled herself into his body and lifted onto her toes the better to reach his mouth. Caelan smiled against her lips and let her hands go, pulling her even closer against his powerful body, his arms tightening across her back.

Sensuous anticipation sizzled like wildfire across her

nerve ends, pierced every cell, throbbed deliciously through her breasts as she instinctively pressed against him, silently demanding satisfaction for the craving that possessed her.

Eyes gleaming fire and ice, he lifted his head. Abby's heart blocked her throat when she saw the stain of colour across his stark cheekbones and the way his face had clamped into a drawn, predatory focus.

On her, she thought, thrilled even as she realised the danger. For once, the control that was so integral a part of him had been stripped away; he wanted her as violently as she desired him—and, although he was fighting it, he wasn't able to defeat the longing. This wild clamour of the senses was entirely mutual, and she was shamelessly, fiercely excited.

CHAPTER TEN

EYES gleaming, Caelan lifted his head. 'What the hell do you do to me?'

The abrasive note in his voice broke into Abby's trance, but only to increase her delicious, reckless response. She slid her hands up his back, relishing the way the muscles flexed beneath her questing palms, the sheer power and strength of his big body, both protective and intensely dangerous.

'It's entirely mutual.' Her husky voice startled her.

'I know.' He cupped her face, his lean fingers exquisitely gentle around the fine bones, his thumbs stroking across her lips to silence her. 'That it affects *you* so profoundly is the only thing that makes *my* weakness endurable,' he said roughly, and kissed her again, this time on the brow and then on each eyelid as it swept down.

Weakness? Oh, yes—divine weakness...

All coherent thought fled when he slid his hands the silken length of her throat. Abby shivered violently at the contrast between the heat of his hands and a rush of cool, salt-scented air across her skin when he undid the buttons of her jacket and pushed it down her arms. The fine material whispered in the silence as it slipped onto the floor.

Somewhere in the dimmest, furthest reaches of Abby's brain a small voice insisted she stop this before it went too far, but she was already lost to the sensuous magic of his nearness.

Everything about him—the subtle scent that was his alone, the way his breathing deepened when he was aroused, his taste in her mouth—alerted long-repressed responses. The bitter ache of loss was rapidly banished by the incandescent pleasure of being held close to his hardening body, of knowing that soon there would be greater pleasure, pleasure piling on pleasure until the final addictive ecstasy of union.

Everything—her heart, her head—disengaged; she forced up her weighted lashes and stared at him with huge, dazed eyes, darkly dilating as his fingers moved across the wisp of silken camisole beneath.

Her pulse stopped until a potent, dangerous excitement drove it into action again. Colour burned along the striking sweep of his arrogant cheekbones, and his eyes were flame-blue, so hot she thought they should burn the pale skin he was examining with all a conqueror's unwavering intentness.

Only who was the conqueror here, who the vanquished? Abby recognised the will-power it took for him to transfer that molten gaze to her face.

'If you really don't want this, tell me to stop. Another heartbeat will be too late,' he warned, for once without his usual crisp delivery.

A deep, insistent craving drove her answer. 'It's too late for me now,' she muttered hoarsely, and took his hand and put it on her breast. Immediately obvious, the pleading, demanding nipple thrust against his palm.

Eyes still locked with hers in a challenge, his hand closed around the soft mound, a thumb rubbing gently across the tip in erotic loveplay.

Arrows of delight pierced her, homing straight and true to the aching emptiness in the pit of her stomach, heating her into slick surrender. She had been lost and was found, safe again after long, lonely weeks. A soft sound, almost a moan, escaped her lips, and she slid her arms beneath his shirt and stood on tiptoe to kiss the tanned skin of his throat, her lips and tongue lingering so she could inhale his scent and taste him.

He froze, his face clamping into a mask of ferocious tension, and then his broad shoulders lifted as he dragged in a deep breath.

'Not here,' he muttered.

But when he lifted her he didn't carry her into the house. The heavily erotic perfume of unknown flowers filled her nostrils as he strode along the terrace, cradling her as though she was the most precious of burdens. When a fold of fabric brushed across her arm she opened her eyes and caught a glimpse of some sort of pavilion, open to the sea, closed by drifting curtains of white on the other three sides. From the corner of her eye she saw a wide couch.

And then Caelan eased her with erotic slowness down his aroused body.

After that nothing else mattered. He slid the filmy camisole over her head and unclipped the bra beneath. Her skin tightened; she should have felt vulnerable standing in front of him naked from the waist up, but enchantment lent her courage.

'You are so beautiful you unman me,' he said with such harsh emphasis her heart rejoiced.

With bold intentness she scrutinised him, and laughed deep in her throat. 'It doesn't look like it,' she said, and stroked lightly, delicately, over the evidence of the effect she had on him.

But when he caught her hand and held it away, her confidence fled, only to return with his words, delivered with tight restraint.

'Do that again and it will all be over,' he said, through clenched teeth. 'I might just be able to control myself if you undress me, but I'm not going to make it if you do any more.'

Excitement burgeoned into fever, summoning a heat that flashed through her like lightning, yet she was shivering and her hands trembled as she unbuttoned his shirt.

She hadn't forgotten how magnificent he was, how the sight of his wide chest and wider shoulders aroused her. She let herself stroke once across his sleek tanned skin, delighting in its warm exotic blend of bronze and gold, but stopped when his ragged intake of breath warned her she was too close to the sensitive nipple.

In a shaken, thick voice he said, 'I'll do the rest.'

Abby didn't trust herself to watch him undress. Instead, she fumbled with the fastener of her skirt, eventually getting herself out of it to stand in nothing but a sexy little suspender belt and the exquisite silk stockings the couturier had insisted on. Her body shook with such keen hunger that she thought she might not be able to stop herself from coming there and then at the sight of him.

So she kept her lashes lowered, only for them to fly up in startled shock when he dropped to his knees in front of her and slid his arms around her hips, kissing the soft indentation of her waist.

Her pulse pounded through her body. Unable to resist, she threaded her hands through the cool silk of his hair, holding him close until he said against her skin, 'If we're going to take these off I need to see what I'm doing.'

She held her breath as he unclipped the suspenders, but when he kissed the fine, satiny skin at the top of her thighs her knees buckled. Lips drawn back in a feral smile, he freed her from the wisp of satin suspender belt and stood up, magnificently naked and openly desirous.

Inside Abby, excitement transformed every nerve impulse into deep-seated craving; her hands clenched and she felt it beat up through her like a bushfire, beautiful beyond compare and ferociously dangerous.

For a few seconds he stood looking down at her, eyes smouldering crystals in his lean, tanned face. 'You're mine,' he said on a guttural note. 'Admit it.'

'Yes,' she conceded, unable to deny him this triumph.

His arms closed around her, clamping her against him so that they came down onto the couch in one smooth, powerful movement. He bent his head to rest his cheek against her breasts.

Abby's heart dissolved. 'And you are mine,' she claimed, her hand against his cheek, thrilling to the soft abrasion against her palm and the sensitive skin he was kissing.

He turned his face and his lips closed on the centre of her breast, and she cried out again, a ragged, wordless utterance of sexual hunger so powerful she couldn't think beyond her acute need for the heady satisfaction only Caelan could give her.

Primitively, she wanted to lie beneath him in complete surrender, to feel the hard thrust of his body as he entered her, to be driven up that slow, passionate rise towards the heights of rapture. And then, when the pleasure became unbearable she'd give him everything, and take from him too as the whole power of his big body clenched in release.

But not yet. Not for long minutes yet...

Slowly, as though every revisited caress, every newly minted sensation, every memory of how it had been for them a month before needed to be coaxed back into life, they explored each other's bodies. Abby could see how difficult it was for him; she knew how tense she was with frustrated desire, yet because this was special she let herself become as absorbed as he was in their journey of rediscovery.

And then, when at last neither could bear it any longer, he eased himself over and into her, watching her face so that he could see every nuance of emotion.

Her breath rasping her throat, Abby lifted her hips and locked her legs around his, pulling him into her as she tightened her arms around him. He gave a muffled groan and every bit of finesse went west. He thrust deeply into her, setting off an explosive release that rocketed her into orgasm. Panting, she felt waves of agonised pleasure catch her up and fling her into ecstasy.

He joined her there, and in that exhilarating final frenzy of physical passion she accepted that she would stay with him, not for all the reasons it made sense—not because he threatened her, not for Michael, but because she needed Caelan on some level that transcended everything else.

Love? She didn't know, and at that moment she didn't much care. It was enough.

And afterwards, it was poignantly sweet to lie in his arms, sweet to listen to the slow recovery of their mingled breaths and pulses, sweet to lie beneath him and feel his beloved weight on her once more. Yet a profound sadness overwhelmed her.

With all this, was she being greedy craving his love? Because that was what had happened. Somehow, in spite of everything, she'd done the unbearable—given him her heart.

Caelan rolled over onto his back and looped a long arm around her, pulling her to lie against him, her body lax and depleted, her face buried against his neck.

After a long time he said, 'Are you using any sort of birth control?'

'No,' she admitted in a voice that seemed to come from a huge distance away.

He said something blood-curdling beneath his breath in a language that had to be Dacian. 'And, idiot that I am, I didn't even think of it.' He tipped up her chin and examined her face, his own speculative. 'Why not?'

She searched for an answer, knowing that there was no good one. 'Like you, I didn't think of it,' she finally confessed. Only she'd had a month to consider it...

'So you might be pregnant right now.'

Oh, to carry Caelan's child under her heart...

Any child would be another chain binding them together to provide security for Michael, she reminded herself, a hostage to make sure she didn't leave this marriage. A child would simply give Caelan more leverage.

'I doubt it,' she said slowly, trying to pull away. His arms tightened around her, and into his neck she muttered, 'I believe it takes even the most virile sperm some time to actually get to the egg.'

But she couldn't suppress a tiny thrill at the thought of that most elemental of journeys happening inside her.

A note in his soft laughter told her that it excited him too. He stroked the curve of her breast, and that primal heat re-ignited in every cell.

Holding her gaze with his own, he said evenly, 'A child would convince everyone that we plan to stay together.'

Even though she'd thought exactly the same thing, to hear it put into words hurt in some obscure fashion. She snapped, 'I'll do a lot for Michael, but I'm damned if I'll have a child for him.'

Caelan said grimly, 'I hope that doesn't mean what it sounds like.'

'What?'

He was watching her, his face hard and purposeful. 'That you'll make sure no child eventuates.'

Abby felt sick. 'No, I won't do that,' she said quietly.

His gaze pierced her, searching into her very soul. 'I believe you.' He smiled when a sudden yawn took her completely by surprise. 'Bedtime, I think.'

He got up, perfectly unconcerned at his nudity, and scooped her up. When she realised he was going to leave the pavilion she blurted, 'What about servants?'

'Don't worry,' he drawled, 'there's nobody here but us.'

He carried her to a room filled with the slow music of the sea. Another bottle of champagne—or perhaps the same one—stood on a table in the window. A huge bed dominated the room.

What now? Abby thought frantically.

'Our clothes have been unpacked,' Caelan told her. He nodded towards a couple of doors. 'The one on the left is your bathroom; the other is mine.'

Two bathrooms? But clearly he intended them to sleep together, and some privacy might help her regain some self-possession. Relieved, she said thinly, 'I'll have a shower,' and escaped into a fantasy bathroom of marble and mirrors and exotic plants, the air heavily scented by the jasmine flowers that had been scattered in the huge, square bath.

Abby caught back a sob. Someone had gone to an enormous amount of trouble to set the scene for their honeymoon!

She welcomed the soothing hiss of cool water over her sensitised skin, then wrapped herself in the sensuous slither of satin she found hanging behind the door, a nightgown in palest green. Where had it come from?

It had to be Caelan; another example of his thoughtfulness—or his experience in romantic encounters. Frowning, she finished her preparations for the night, but before she'd removed the cosmetics from her face her speculation was replaced by pain.

Of course she'd fallen in love with him! Who was she to think she could succeed in keeping her heart inviolate when so many other women, sophisticated and worldly, had failed?

He must never know. All she had to cling to was her pride, and that would be shattered in humiliation if he knew she'd surrendered far more than her body to him.

The room was empty when she returned, but he came in shortly after her, devastating in a black wrap that emphasised the smooth, powerful flow of his body beneath the thin silk.

'Champagne?' he asked after a swift, keen glance that seemed to strip through the fragile protective skin she'd erected.

She shook her head. 'No, thank you. Caelan, who has gone to such trouble for us?'

'Trouble?'

Awkwardly she gestured at the exquisite garment she wore. 'This nightgown isn't mine,' she said, 'and my bath was scattered with flowers—some kind of jasmine, I think.'

'The gown is yours,' he said coolly. 'And the jasmine flowers would be the idea of the housekeeper. You can thank her tomorrow morning.'

'I'll do that,' she said, adding with stiff formality, 'And thank you for the gown.'

'You look like something wild from the woods,' he remarked, coming towards her.

Abby's heart started hammering in her chest. She couldn't move, couldn't do anything but let herself be captured by his dark sexuality. When he held out his hand she took it and let him draw her to the bed.

Later—much later—she listened to his breathing in the darkness and wondered wearily what was going to happen now. Exhaustion, physical and mental, dragged her down, yet she couldn't get to sleep.

Right from the start she'd known that his objective was—and a very fine one, too—to make Michael happy. She wasn't anything more than a necessary evil, albeit one he wanted.

Why couldn't she accept what he offered without longing for more?

She lay looking into an unbearable future until dawn; only then, to the sound of birds carolling, did she slide into exhausted sleep.

She woke to the scent of jasmine, and the sound of a telephone ringing at some distance.

'What the—?' she groaned, jackknifing upwards. She stared blankly at the curtains and pushed a tangle of hair back from her face. By the position of the sun it had to be mid-morning. God, she was making a habit of this!

Caelan's voice—deep and deliberate, textured in intimidating shades of authority—brought back the previous night. Erotic memories swamped her, so potent she had to fight back the instinct to cower under the bedclothes. If only it were that easy to hide! Last night she'd surrendered everything to the compulsion of passion, and been ruthlessly shown the limits of her will-power; now she had to face the consequences.

She pushed back the sheet and swung her feet onto the floor at the moment that Caelan walked in through a wall of shuttered glass doors. Fully dressed, he was carrying a tray.

Perched on the edge of the bed with the sleek satin nightgown rumpled around her thighs, she felt intensely vulnerable. She caught his raised brows as he took in her immodest covering, and, hot with embarrassment, swung her legs up onto the bed and hauled the sheet over them.

His smile told her she needn't have bothered, that he remembered everything of their fevered love-making the previous night.

'You didn't stir when I looked in earlier,' Caelan said, his voice amused and silkily reminiscent, 'so I decided to let you sleep as long as you could.'

Abby fought back another wave of humiliation. No doubt he thought he had her exactly where he wanted her—besotted! 'Thank you,' she said tonelessly. 'But I can be ready for breakfast in ten minutes.'

'It's all right,' he said with cool irony that made her feel stupid, and put the tray on the bedside table.

When she tensed, he smiled and bent to kiss her, his lips warm and seducing. In spite of everything, her mouth softened under his.

But when Caelan straightened, he looked down at her with burnished eyes as cold as a polar star.

'It's too late for second thoughts,' he said implacably. 'We've been married twice, and Michael is safe. I made vows; like you, I keep my promises.'

'I'm not having second thoughts.' Her voice was every bit as determined as his.

He held her gaze for several long moments, then nodded. 'Eat up. And then see if you can sleep some more. I'm afraid that I have work to do, but I'll see you in a couple of hours.'

Watching him go, Abby bit her lip. So much for last night's wild passion; today he was all business. Although the change hurt some newly sensitive part of herself, she forced down as much of the breakfast as she could, then hastily showered, skin scorching when she discovered the marks of their loving on it. No bruising—he had been exquisitely tender with her—but soft abrasions from his beard.

And her slow, deep tiredness wasn't all because of her lack of sleep—it went right down to her bones, and came from exhilarating sexual satiation.

She explored a little of the garden, but didn't like to go too far; it seemed an intrusion. When Caelan found her she was reading out on the terrace.

He gave her a narrow glance, then said, 'You forgot these,' and tossed her a handful of fire.

'What—*oh*!' She caught the rings automatically. Last night she'd taken them off and left them on the bedside cabinet.

'Put them on,' he said shortly.

Her heart heavy, she slid them onto her finger. They meant so much to her—and so little to Caelan. This, after all, was a sensible marriage, entered into for entirely practical reasons.

She looked up and caught Caelan's kindling glance; well, perhaps not entirely practical, she conceded. But what would happen when he was sated with her?

CHAPTER ELEVEN

'HOME again!' Michael announced, beaming with pleasure when the car drew up in the reserved parking slot beneath the hotel. He turned to the woman beside him and said, 'Here we are, Nanny! Home again!'

Relief warred with unease in Abby. She'd been ambivalent when Caelan suggested that Ilana accompany them back to New Zealand, but she had to admit that the nursemaid's help had made the plane trip back from Dacia less tiring. Between them all, Michael was kept busy and happy.

Perhaps it was a good thing the four days of their honeymoon, a jumble of vivid images that still brought the colour to her cheeks, a blur of sun and sea and passionate love-making, had been superseded by the long flight back to New Zealand.

Not love—*sex*, she reminded herself astringently. There'd been no love in Caelan's expertise, just a huge natural understanding of the pleasure points in a woman's body and a compelling masculinity that transformed her desire into a pulsing beat of reckless hunger.

And experience—lots and lots of experience. Put crudely, Caelan was a stud. He knew how to pleasure a woman, how to make her sob with longing and scream with ecstasy and eventually sate her of everything but the need to sleep in his arms.

The silence in the car recalled her to her surroundings. Caelan was looking down at her, his eyes gleaming and his mouth curved in a smile that sent a sensual shiver down her backbone. He couldn't know what she was thinking, but she'd better thrust those memories into the darkest recesses of her mind before she gave herself away.

It seemed incredible that she'd wondered when Caelan would get tired of her.

Early days yet, she thought cynically.

Not that she had much time to worry. Over breakfast the day after they arrived back in New Zealand he said, 'When is a good time for you to see a land agent?'

'Me? What for?'

'I'm feeling dynastic,' he said with a sardonic smile. 'We need a house, and you should choose it. I deal with one agent—my PA will make an appointment for her to call on you.'

'Any time.' She hid an odd pang of pleasure with her cool tone.

With a swift, unreadable glance he said, 'You'll manage.'

His assurance of her ability boosted her confidence, but she had to ask, 'What sort of house do you want?'

He leaned back and surveyed her. 'That's for you to decide. Do you want to live in Auckland, or would you rather be out in the country?'

They discussed it for some minutes, eventually deciding on a place with room for the pony Michael wanted, and then Caelan said, 'We have invitations to deal with. I've already accepted one—it's a dinner for a charity I'm interested in. White tie, so you'll need a suitable outfit.' He frowned. 'Your credit card should have arrived; I'll check the mail.'

She bit her lip. Common sense told her that she had to have some income, but she felt sullied, like a kept woman.

Of course he noticed. 'I've already paid your allowance into your account. We can discuss the rest of the invitations over tonight. Are you all right to stay with Cia and Hunt next weekend?'

'Yes.'

He gave her another keen, too-perceptive scrutiny. 'I thought you liked them.'

'I do, very much.'

'But?'

Of course he wouldn't let it go. She said diffidently, 'I'm not a huge party person, Caelan.'

'Nor I,' he returned promptly. 'Don't fret about our social life. You'll find your feet. Oh, by the way, I've been contacted by at least four magazines for interviews. Do you want to do them?'

Abby shuddered. 'No, thanks.'

He grinned, but said, 'I'd already refused, so even if you'd longed to adorn their pages your hard, dictatorial husband would have forbidden it. And the social welfare caseworker has been in touch. She'll call in to see us tomorrow afternoon.' His voice altered. 'Just be careful when you're out and about. There's been a lot of publicity, unfortunately, and it wouldn't surprise me if you're the target of photographers.'

She said gloomily, 'Three months ago I'd never have believed that I'd have to dodge paparazzi.'

Or kidnappers. That still didn't seem possible in New Zealand, but whenever she or Michael went out a man who doubled as chauffeur was close behind.

'The fuss will die down,' Caelan said coolly.

And indeed, after a couple of weeks of embarrassing attention, an All Black player was discovered to be having an affair with his brother's wife, and the media's interest switched abruptly.

The appointment with the caseworker—and the several subsequent ones—went well. Michael showed off on his jungle gym with every appearance of delight, introduced his nanny with pride, and chattered brightly about his new friends at the pre-school.

On the surface, she and Caelan settled easily into a life together, sharing Michael without too many significant silences. Occasionally their good humour stretched thin, but both made valiant efforts not to let underlying tension impinge on the third member of the family.

But although the sex remained wonderful and Caelan's support gave her the confidence to deal well with the various glittering social occasions they attended, a bleak sense of isolation robbed her days of delight and joy.

Nevertheless, she enjoyed the weekend with Lucia and Hunt on his huge cattle station. They weren't the only guests; she soon realised she'd been introduced to a tight-knit social circle that rarely appeared in the gossip columns. She and another woman, also from Auckland, discovered they had much in common.

After that she lunched with Peta McIntosh several times. Forthright and sensible and completely in love with her gorgeous husband, Peta had run her own farm. Abby hoped they were working their way towards friendship. It had been a long time since she'd had a good woman friend.

Soon the halcyon days in Dacia faded into a memory of pageantry and old-world fairy tale as Abby flung herself into the search for the perfect house. Michael blossomed, exercising every muscle in his sturdy, compact body on the gym bars, swimming, and teaching his nursemaid all the English nursery rhymes and stories he knew, while unconsciously absorbing Dacian from her.

Most afternoons his uncle came home early from work

to play with him, and their relationship prospered. But after dinner each night Caelan worked from the office in the apartment, and several times he flew to various places around the Pacific for meetings. He didn't ask Abby to go with him, but he did ring every evening.

Always he brought home gifts—amusing novelties for Michael, a New Zealand dictionary for Ilana.

For Abby there were golden pearls from Tahiti, an exquisite silk kimono from Japan, and after a trip to Australia he slipped a dress ring onto her finger, a glittering square-cut golden diamond surrounded by smaller ones.

'Yes, I thought it was the same colour as your eyes,' he said, and kissed her with controlled passion.

His thoughtfulness, his casual generosity, hurt her. Oddly, it seemed to emphasise that their relationship was a fake.

Forget about any meeting of minds, any emotional commitment. It wasn't love Caelan felt, merely its mindless brother, lust. She'd tried to trick it out in the panoply of love, but it was time to face the truth.

She'd stay safe if she didn't expect too much from this marriage or this man, she cautioned that romantic, hungry part of herself. But in spite of her attempts to grow a skin over her emotions, she couldn't stop herself from falling more and more in love with her husband each day.

Although he didn't want her love, his need for her body didn't fade; each night she surrendered to an ever-increasing hunger, flaming in his arms, but when it was over she wondered despairingly how she was going to keep her soul intact.

Previously she'd envied his iron control, preserved even when they'd made love. But that had been when she thought there must be something warmer behind it.

Now she was discovering in the most painful way possible that control was all he had.

Once, lying in his arms, she'd blurted, 'Have you ever been drunk?'

His brows rose. 'I admit to my fair share of the usual adolescent excesses,' he said blandly. 'Yes, I've been drunk. I didn't like it, and I don't plan to do it again.'

It figured, she thought savagely.

About a month after they arrived back he said casually just before he left for work, 'Are you busy today?'

Carefully composing her expression, Abby looked up from watching Michael do acrobatics on his gym bars. 'This morning I'm going out to Clevedon to look at a property the agent thinks might be suitable, but after that I'm free.'

'Meet me at the office and we'll have lunch together.'

Her foolish heart sped up. They'd never been on a date. 'I—well, yes, I'd love that.' And because the amused glint in his eyes made her self-conscious, she added primly, 'Thank you.'

He bent and dropped a swift, disturbing kiss on her mouth. 'I'll see you at one, then.'

At one she was in a private waiting room in his office reading a magazine when the skin between her shoulder blades tingled and her heartbeat sped up. Slowly she turned her head. Caelan stood in the doorway, tall and dark and dangerous in his superbly cut suit, examining her with narrowed eyes. He wasn't smiling.

'You look fantastic,' he said calmly. 'Hungry?'

'More than ready,' she admitted, pleased in spite of herself at the easy compliment. 'I've spent the morning tramping around a farm.'

'Any good?'

'I didn't like the house much—too heavily formal.' She frowned. 'Sometimes I think I'm too fussy.'

'Perhaps we should discuss building a house for ourselves. Forget about it for now, though.'

She'd expected to eat at a restaurant, but in the lift reserved for him he pressed a button and they shot upwards. 'Where are we going?' she asked.

'To a private dining room,' he told her calmly.

The lift slowed and stopped—only one floor up, she noted.

She gave him a startled glance. 'Why do we need privacy?'

His broad shoulders moved in the superbly tailored jacket and his eyes were bland and noncommittal. 'I have something to tell you. I don't want to risk being overheard.' He opened the door and ushered her into a small foyer.

Stomach clenching, she said, 'What?'

He looked down through his lashes, eyes gleaming like blue crystals, but silently opened a door and stepped back. 'Come in.'

'Said the spider to the fly.' Tension tightened her skin, but she made a show of looking around the large space he escorted her into, half sitting room, the other half occupied by an already-set table.

'A very beautiful fly,' Caelan returned smoothly.

It was another superficial, meaningless compliment; Abby knew very well that she wasn't beautiful. 'Thank you,' she said tonelessly.

Being Caelan, he didn't leave it at that. 'You don't believe me?' he drawled.

She shrugged. 'Striking is probably the most apt word for me—and then only because of my hair.' She didn't give him time to answer. Concentrating on shoring up her fragile façade, she asked, 'What is this place?'

'It's an apartment used by executives from overseas.' And by him when he needed privacy. He indicated the table, already set with silver and wineglasses and flowers. 'Come and sit down.'

'Where does the food come from?'

'The restaurant on the ground floor.' He held out a chair for her, and, once she sat down, pushed it in.

He was treating her like a guest. Yet in spite of her apprehension her body tingled and the low, subliminal throb of desire warmed her cheeks beneath the soft haze of blusher. His hands lingered on her shoulders, just long enough for the heat burning through her to turn feral.

'You forgot your skin,' he said calmly.

'What?'

It suddenly seemed very stupid for her to be here alone with him. Over the past weeks Michael and Ilana had acted as emotional chaperones, reminding them why they'd embarked on this masquerade marriage.

Here, on neutral ground, his fingers resting lightly on the silken skin of her neck, every sense quivering with the pleasure of his closeness, bold, consuming desire clamoured up through her like a summons, utterly elemental and reckless.

Was this planned?

Oh, almost certainly. Did she care?

Not at this minute, she thought, and thrilled to the knowledge.

Only to deflate when Caelan stepped back.

Shielding her dilating pupils with her lashes, she surveyed him as he sat down opposite her. The carnal need smouldering in her noted the stripped, fierce prominence of his facial structure, telling her he was as aware of her as she was of him. And his eyes were lit with blue fire, diamond-bright and intense.

'What did you mean—I forgot my skin?' Shocked and startled by the languid drift of the words, she folded her lips into a firm, straight line.

He let his gaze roam her face. 'You said it was your hair that makes you stand out. It helps, but you have skin like luminous gold silk. And your eyes are tilted enough to give you an air of mystery. Then you smile, and it's Circe all over again, an enchantress turning men into swine with that mocking smile.'

He spoke with cool detachment, and her heart froze in horror. Was that how he saw her—or himself? Did he despise himself for wanting her?

'Until I say something and reveal a perfectly ordinary woman,' she said, blundering along as best she could when her insides were churning.

Yet she was glad he'd said it. They'd never explored their deepest emotions and values. Oh, they'd discussed politics and music and art; they'd made love like tigers, fiercely and with such passion that it temporarily eased the ache in her heart, but love was founded on knowledge and understanding, not the primeval recklessness of sexual hunger.

He frowned. 'Ordinary? Far from it,' he said drily. '*Ordinary* women don't commit themselves to felony and poverty to keep a promise made to a woman who had no right to extract it.'

A subdued hum of activity through a door into the next room stopped her swift rebuttal, but when the waiter had left Abby said, 'Whether she had reason or not, Gemma was desperate. And I don't regret anything I did for Michael.' She looked down and added painfully, 'What I do regret is that you missed his first years. It's no excuse, but I truly didn't think you'd be interested in him. Gemma's fears influenced me, and I'd like to believe that the horror of what happened to her unhinged me temporarily. I should have done things differently.'

The silence that followed was almost too much to bear. In the end she glanced up, and met hooded eyes in a lean, arrested face.

She said hurriedly, 'You're so good with him, and he already loves you and trusts you. He's missed out on knowing you, and you've missed out too. I wish I'd contacted you—although I'd have fought you to a standstill when you tried to gain custody.'

Caelan said slowly, 'Actually, that's what I brought you here to talk about.'

She froze. 'What do you mean?'

'I've been contacted by the writer who was doing a book on tragedies of the South Pacific.'

Tender, delicious asparagus turned to ashes in her mouth. Eyes dilating, she stared at him as the colour drained from her face. 'And?' she managed.

'I've met him. He's done his research.' He spoke dispassionately. 'He knows that you claimed Michael for your own child.'

Her fork clattered onto the tablecloth. 'Oh, God!' But before he could speak, she said urgently, 'Caelan, it doesn't matter. In a way, I'll be glad to have it out in the open. And if I do get prosecuted and—and convicted, then I know you'll look after Michael.'

'Don't worry—he won't mention anything beyond the fact that Michael is now our son.'

'What?' She dragged in a jagged breath.

'You're my wife,' he said, as though that explained it. Shaken and sickened, she bit her lip. Of course he wouldn't want his wife—Michael's mother—to be sent to prison. 'I'm sorry.'

'You did what you felt was best for Michael.' His voice was cool, almost indifferent. 'And you were right; nursemaids don't have the same emotional investments in their charges as mothers. Michael is open and loving and happy, and he's secure in your love. He likes Ilana very much, but he runs to you when he hurts himself.'

Warmed though she was by his acceptance, she said miserably, 'But what's to stop this writer from black-mailing you again? Because I assume that's what he did.'

He said austerely, 'I don't blackmail easily. But he didn't even try; he simply wanted to make sure that he didn't make an enemy by revealing something I didn't want generally known. So, you see, that power and money and influence you so rightly despise have some advantages.' His smile was a masterpiece of sardonic acceptance. 'It appears I have a reputation for being a bad enemy.'

She could believe that. Choosing her words carefully, she said, 'I only despise power and influence and money that's used to harm people.'

Caelan said crisply, 'I'm glad to hear it. Forget about the writer; he's not going to spill the beans. When he contacted me I got in touch with my solicitor, who said it was highly unlikely you'd be prosecuted. And once Michael is legally our child you'll be safe, especially as you've shown yourself to be an excellent mother. So you've no reason to worry.'

'I'm not,' she said, and realised it was true. She picked up the glass of wine she hadn't touched, and sipped a small amount, then asked something that *had* been concerning her. 'Is it possible that Gemma's mother might want access to Michael?'

'She didn't want access to her own child,' he returned caustically, 'so why would she be interested in her grandson?' He gave her a shrewd glance. 'But if it eases that tender heart of yours, once the adoption is signed, sealed and delivered, we'll contact her and let her know.'

Abby looked at her plate, then back at him. 'I was never happy with the promise I made Gemma,' she said quietly, 'but I had to keep it.'

His brows lifted. 'I know that now. The woman I thought you were would have sold him to me. And as this is confession time, I'll admit that you were right to be scathing about my supposed plans for Michael when I arrived in Nukuroa.'

'*Supposed?*' she asked sharply.

'In reality I'd planned to set you and Michael up in a house in the suburbs in Auckland.' His mouth slanted in self-derision. 'I'd already bought a pleasant place with a garden in Titirangi. You'd have liked it—lots of trees for Michael to climb and lawns to run across. I intended to see him several times a week, have him sleep over with me when he got to know me—'

'And take him from me when he did know you!' she interrupted fiercely.

He shrugged, his mouth compressed. 'Yes. I didn't intend to let either him or you impinge on my life much.'

Something broke inside Abby. Panting, her voice low and furious, she snarled, 'You accused me of playing with Michael's life. Didn't it occur to you that you were doing exactly the same thing?'

'Yes.'

Scornfully she demanded, 'So what made you change your mind?'

His brows lifted. 'I told myself it was revenge.'

Silence followed the ugly word, dark as a storm with

unspoken thoughts and emotions. Every inchoate suspicion, every dark wondering moment, came back to haunt her.

In a dead voice she said, 'So you used the one thing I wanted, to stay with Michael, to force me into marriage.' Her chin came up and she stared at him accusingly, eyes wide and unblinking as a cat's. 'Is this where you tell me that you're going to divorce me?'

Blue eyes glittering, he demanded, 'Is that what you think?'

'What else can I think?' So angry and despairing she could barely articulate, she flung the words at him like bullets, knowing even as she spoke that it was useless. 'It would be the perfect revenge!'

His mirthless bark of laughter shocked her. He said between his teeth, 'Only if you loved me.'

She stared at him, and then closed her eyes, because of course he knew. Oh, the perfect revenge, she realised in bitter despair. Show a glimpse of paradise, and then snatch it away.

'Well?' he demanded.

She said thinly, 'What?'

'Damn it, Abby, I love you!' He spoke in a goaded voice that was unlike Caelan's confident tones.

Sometimes she'd dreamed of him saying that, and always she'd been ecstatic, filled with reciprocal delight and love. Now she felt empty, as though disillusion had ripped the heart from her body and left her with nothing but hollowness in its place.

A hollowness that wasn't filled when he said roughly, 'Of course I don't want a divorce.'

He couldn't have chosen a way to hurt her more. She longed with every atom in her body to give in, take what he could give and pretend to believe that they could somehow forge a life together. Forcing herself to look him in the eyes, she said brokenly, 'If you think I'm going to be like your father, so desperately in love that I'll put up with anything you want to dish out, you can think again. I'd rather die!'

His eyes glittered. 'Abby, listen to me! I love you.' And when she stared at him he said furiously, 'I can't live without you. I would die for you.'

Her throat locked. She could only stare at him with enormous eyes, her lips trembling. 'I don't believe it.'

'Believe it, if you believe nothing else.'

'Why?'

He paused, as though her question startled him. She saw self-control shutter his eyes against her, clamp his features into a ruthless mask. Panic kicked her in the stomach; she'd been an utter idiot! Far better to have said nothing, to shore up her defences and retain some tatters of pride.

Unable to stand it any longer, she scrambled to her feet. 'Everything you've just told me indicates that you'll never trust me. What sort of love is that? Useless.'

A muscle flicked above his angular jawbone and the white line around his lips made her realise that she'd gone too far. He covered the distance between them in a silent, predatory lunge that drove adrenalin through her in a desperate flood. She swung around, but he caught her by the wrist before she could take more than one step and pulled her to face him.

For the first time ever she looked at him and saw the man without the mask, his eyes narrowed slits of blue, glittering cold as diamonds between black lashes, his mouth compressed into a thin line, real emotion blazing through.

'And you love me,' he said, his lips barely moving,

and when she stared at him, colour firing up through her skin, he laughed deep in his throat and drew her into his arms in a movement that reminded her of the times she'd danced with him.

'No,' she whispered, shaking so much she thought she'd fall if it weren't for his strong arms around her.

'No what? No, you don't love me? Don't lie, Abby, you just admitted it when you said you'd rather die than live in an unequal relationship like my father.' He brushed her lips with his, tantalising her with the light pressure, so erotic she had to close her eyes against him.

But that only made things worse; she couldn't see, but she could smell the faint scent of their arousal and feel the hard strength of his body against hers. Her body clamoured for release and she had no idea what he'd just said, what she'd said, anything at all but the fact that she loved this man with everything she was, had loved him since the first time she'd set eyes on him.

And then she was free and above the chattering of her teeth she heard him say in a raw voice, 'Abby, don't cry. It's all right—you can do whatever you want to do. Just don't cry. I'm not worth it.'

She opened eyes magnified by brimming tears, and said on a sob, 'You're worth so much more, you idiot!'

A wry smile curved his mouth. He reached out a hand and slowly, knowing she was ceding much more than a simple handclasp, she put hers in it. He kissed her fingers, and then in a gesture that twisted her heart he held the palm to his face, and said, 'Is it too late to start again? Properly, this time?'

And this time she believed him. She'd glimpsed the vulnerability behind his intimidating authority, and it had shaken her to her heart. 'It's not too late,' she said softly, with trembling lips.

He held her eyes, his own gaze dark and intense, but not as intense as his voice when he said, 'Do you know when I realised that I loved you?'

Stunned delight shafted through her, rendering her mute. She shook her head.

'On Dacia, the night of our wedding, when you told me indignantly that, although you loved Michael, you wouldn't have a baby for him.' His voice deepened. 'That's when I wondered if it was possible you loved me, because you didn't say you wouldn't have a baby for me. I didn't think I could ever love anyone, but at that moment I felt as though someone had hit me in the heart.' His voice deepened. 'Talk about Cupid's arrows—it was as quick and unexpected as that. One second I didn't know that what I felt for you was love. The next I did. I realised that I wanted to wake up next to you all the mornings of my life.'

It sounded like a vow. She stared at him, then opened her mouth to speak.

A long forefinger closed her lips, signalling that he hadn't finished. Voice very low and sure, he said, 'I've loved you for all my life, it seems. Certainly since well before we were married. I wouldn't face it because I thought being in control of my life was more important than love.' His voice roughened. 'I was wrong.'

Abby gazed into his face, her eyes enormous and questing. What she saw there made sky-rockets go off inside her in mute, overwhelming joy. He gave her a wicked smile, and her last resistance melted, evaporated like rain on a hot summer's day, drifting away into nothingness. She kissed the finger across her mouth.

His eyes flared electric blue, but he shook his head. 'Let me say this now. Although I loved Gemma, and I grieved for her, you have no idea how I felt when I found out that you were still alive. But you'd stolen her child, and I hated you. It was simpler.'

Abby put her hand on his arm, feeling the muscles clench beneath her fingertips. 'She loved you too. Truly. Would you have tried to find me if I hadn't had Michael?'

'Yes,' he said simply. 'Even when I saw the first photograph of you imitating a mouse, your glorious hair straightened and dull, those appalling spectacles hiding your cat-shaped eyes, I must have suspected that it was only a matter of time before I'd love you.'

'You were an utter beast,' she said, believing at last.

'I was fighting a battle with myself,' he said quietly. 'You made a promise to Gemma, and you'd carried it out as best you could. Everything you've done you've done for Michael, and you had every reason to believe that he'd be far better off with you than with me.'

'I was wrong,' she said quietly, 'and so was Gemma. You love him already.'

He shrugged. 'He's a great little kid.'

'You told me he needed a man in his life and I was very scornful, but you were right. He's opened out— become much more of a little boy since we've been here.' She paused, then added, 'And he loves you too.'

A stain of colour emphasised his splendid cheekbones. 'He's a sunny-natured child.' He looked down at her and the passion that had been simmering beneath the surface while they talked flamed up into his eyes, heating them to crystalline fire. 'I'm sorry for hurting you; I'm sorry I was such an idiot that I couldn't recognise what I felt for you. I thought I'd made you resent me so much that the only way to bind you to me was with sex.'

She smiled at him, her almond eyes lazy and languorous, her mouth subtly beckoning. 'I enjoyed that immensely, but I loved you before we made love. I refused to admit it too, so let's not blame each other.'

Potent desire rushed through Caelan, a paradoxical mixture of fierce tenderness. Laughing, his eyes gleaming, he picked her up and held her high in his arms. 'Do you want to finish your lunch?' he asked.

'Somehow I'm not hungry for food any more,' she said demurely, adding with a fascinating upwards glance from beneath her lashes, 'Is there a bed close by?'

'A large, executive-size bed just through that door,' he told her. With the urgent hunger of a lover, he carried her into the adjoining room, and into the rest of their lives together, with complete confidence in their mutual love.

Settling a score—and winning a wife!

Don't miss favorite author Trish Morey's brand-new duet

Part one: Stolen by the Sheikh

Sapphire Clemenger is designing the wedding gown for Sheikh Khaled Al-Ateeq's chosen bride. Sapphy must accompany the prince to his exotic desert palace, and is forbidden to meet his future wife. She begins to wonder if this woman exists....

**Part two: The Mancini Marriage Bargain
Coming in March 2006**

www.eHarlequin.com

If you enjoyed what you just read,
then we've got an offer you can't resist!

Take 2 bestselling
love stories FREE!
Plus get a FREE surprise gift!